I0822258

The Wildegrove Witch

Darkling Souls 2.5

Alex Bree

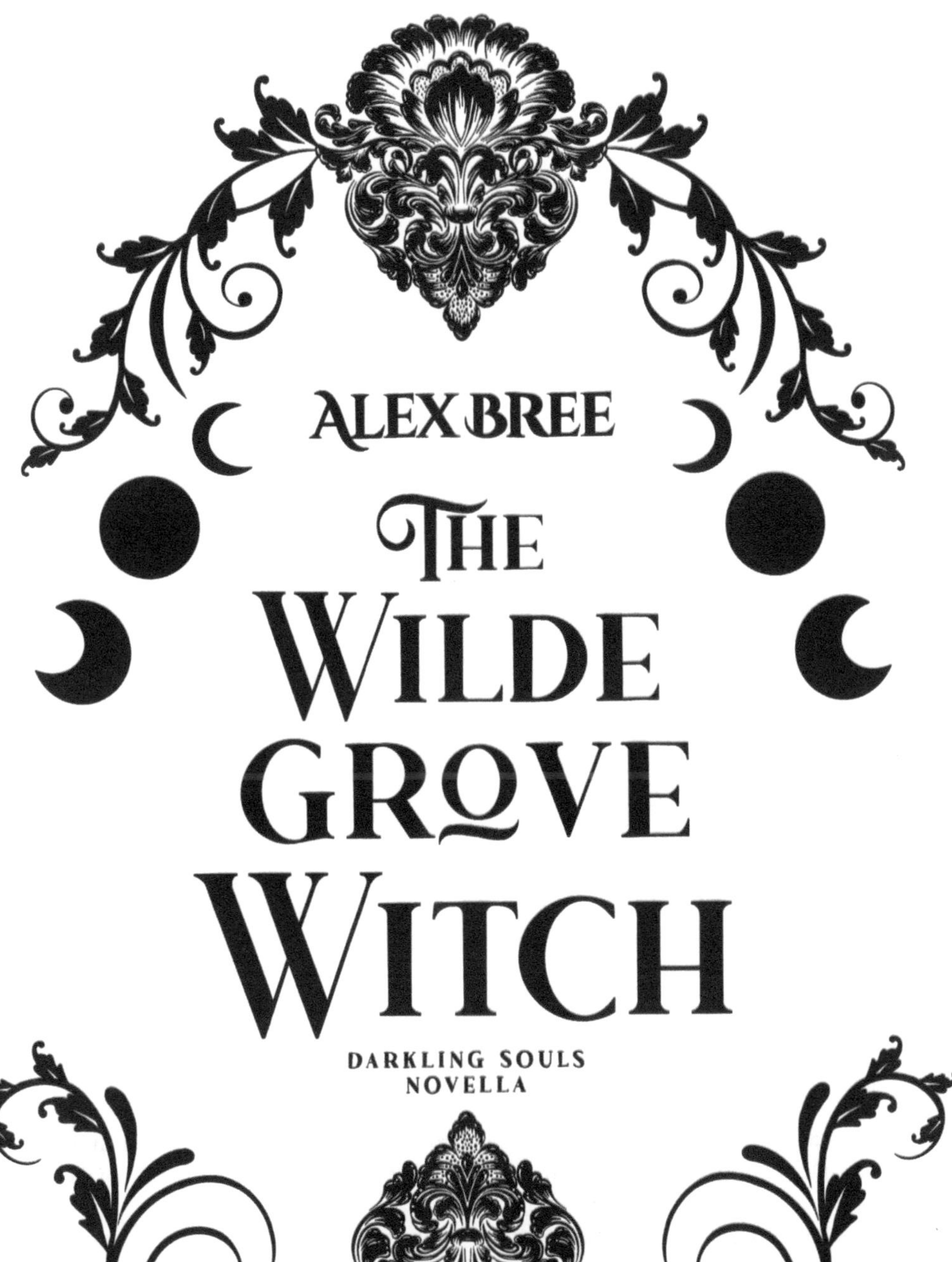

ALEX BREE

THE WILDE GROVE WITCH

DARKLING SOULS
NOVELLA

Cover Art by AC Graphics

Map Art by Alex Bree

First Edition: August 2025

ISBN 9798988373155 (hardcover)

ASIN B0FGKPGXBD (ebook)

CONTENT WARNING

This is a dark fantasy story about monsters with content that may not be suitable for all readers. For a complete content list, please visit the author's website at www.alexbreewrites.com.

DARKLING SOULS READING ORDER

The High Seer (1)
The Nameless Shadow Novella (1.5)
The Queensblood Crown (2)
The Wildegrove Witch Novella (2.5)

THE CONTINENT OF
TERIDAR
Amaryllis
Rexila
The Lost Pass
Warden's Watch Mts.
Avyllon
Brookhaven
Terre Isthmus
Oakwood
Karme
Fangmour
Wildegrove
Wyndsel
Heartspring
Hunger's Teeth Mts.
Warrior's Weald
Sunfyre
Rodarri
Bloodrose Spires
Seven Forests
Titan Cliffs

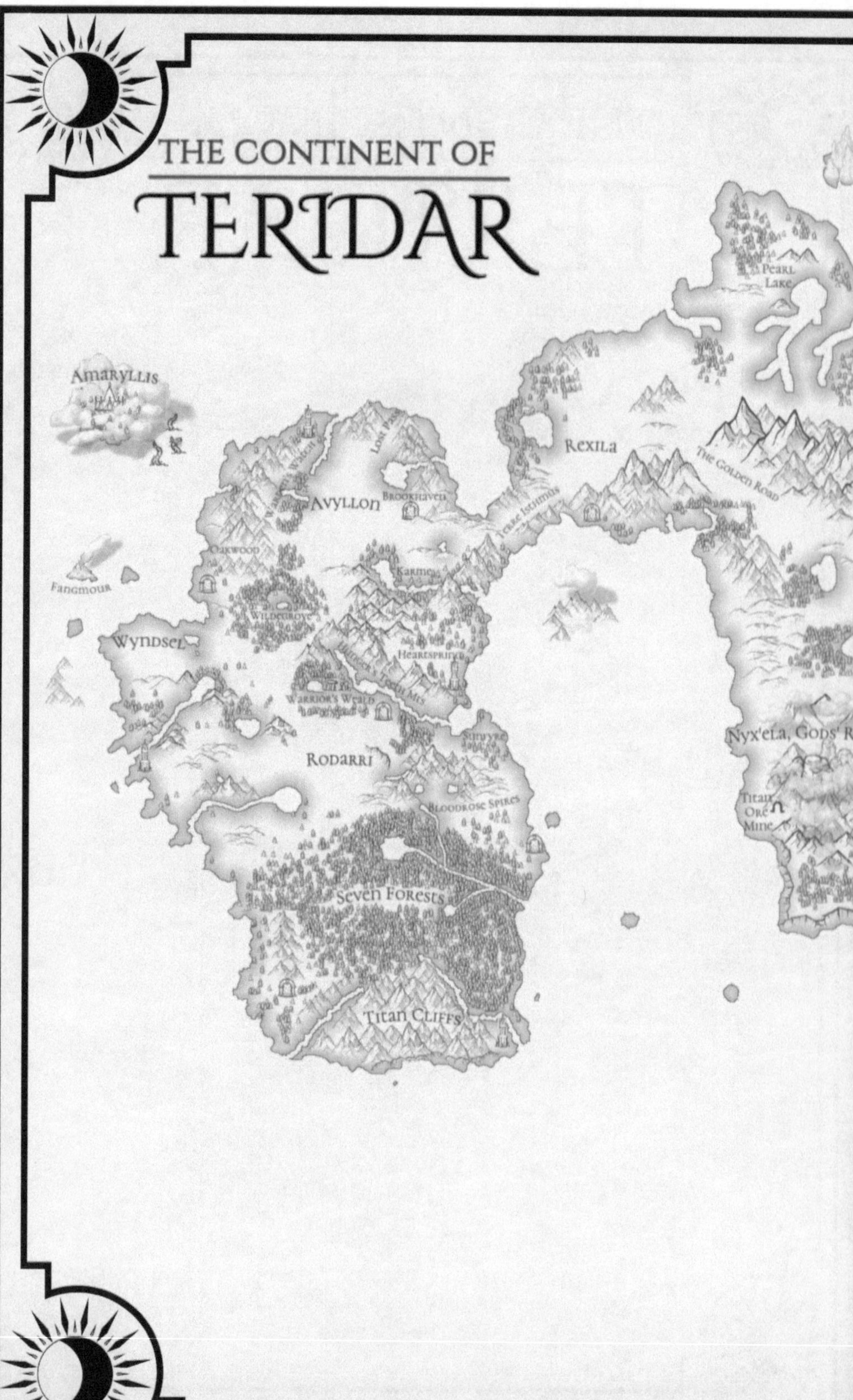
The Continent of
Teridar
Amaryllis
Fangmour
Wyndsel
Avyllon
Lost Pass
Brookhaven
Oakwood
Heartspring
Warrior's Weald
Rodarri
Bloodrose Spires
Seven Forests
Titan Cliffs
Rexila
Terre Isthmus
The Golden Road
Pearl Lake
Nyx'eLa, Gods' Re
Titan Ore Mine

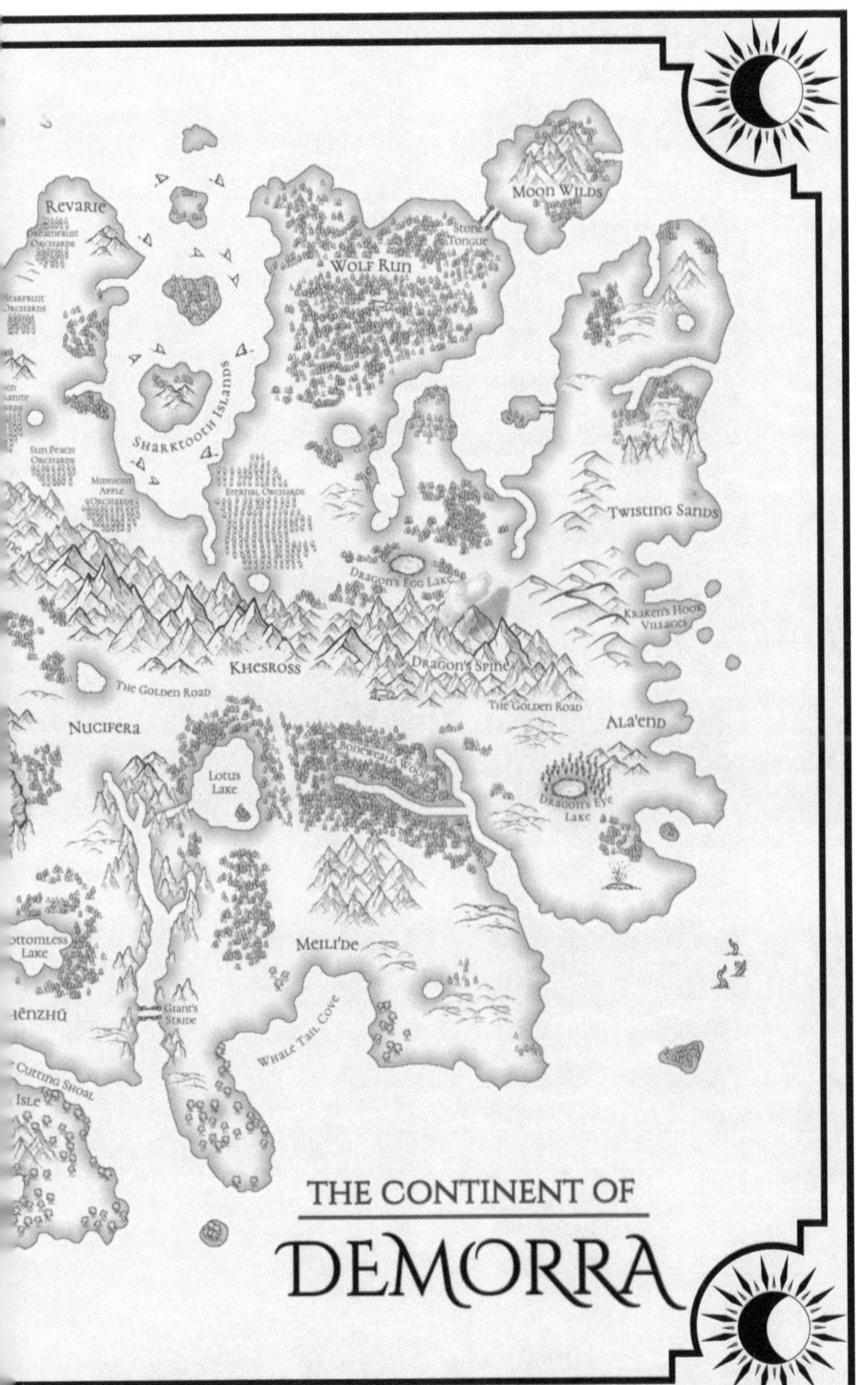

Revarie
Dreamfruit Orchards
Sharktooth Islands
Sun Peach Orchards
Midnight Apple Orchards
Eternal Orchards
Wolf Run
Stone Tongue
Moon Wilds
Twisting Sands
Dragon's Egg Lake
Kraken's Hook Villages
Khesross
Dragon's Spine
The Golden Road
The Golden Road
Ala'end
Nucifera
Lotus Lake
Boneweald Wood
Dragon's Eye Lake
Meili'de
Giant's Stride
Whale Tail Cove
Cutting Shoal
THE CONTINENT OF
DEMORRA

Prologue

All battles are of the heart.

— *Unknown.*

1153 N.T.C. The Flame Pillar.

Clutching the protection charm at her throat, Kassia slipped her hand in her healer's bag so she could grasp whichever potion she needed at a moment's notice as she picked a path through the blood-splattered fields. Destruction marred every inch of the land as far as the eye could see, and she suddenly wished she'd been here to help with the battle. Blast rings and melted glass from sorcerers' alchemical reactions dotted the valley beside crumbling siege towers and war machines. Bending down, she pressed her fingers into the dirt, sensing for the roots deep below. Even the trees and grasses were crying out in agony in the wake of the violence. She sent a comforting burst of magic in reply before standing to let her surroundings wash over her.

Angry tears ran down her face in an unending stream. When Avyllon had called for aid in the aftermath of the Battle for the Flame Pillar, Kassia hadn't realized what she'd been volunteering for. She couldn't have known that *this* was even possible. Despite having fought monsters and sorcerers, the sheer scale of this place was overwhelming. Thousands had found their final resting place here. Avyllon's seers, in their white and golden robes, and bloodwitches in red gowns, lay slain next to the soldiers they'd hoped to protect. Even their vampires had finally been overwhelmed by the sheer force of their foes.

May the ancestors help us all.

Kassia ground her teeth as she noticed a carved face on the mound of stones just a few paces away—the emperor had sent in giant basalt constructs. Beside them, she found the corpses of lithe creatures as tall as trees with scales on their backs, fur on their chests, and feathered wings. Behemoths? The Shadows had been bad enough, but now monsters of old?

And for what? So much needless death and so many families ripped apart for reasons she didn't even understand.

Across the plain, Avyllonian and Rodarrian soldiers searched for any survivors while dispatching remaining enemy Demorrans. Seers, witches, and healers carried the wounded toward large tents. She hurried in their direction. If she could assist, maybe she could drown out the horrors surrounding her. The dried mud crunched under her boots as she strode across the battlefield to where her allies worked. The ground gave way, and she slid, nearly losing her balance.

Kassia covered her nose with her dress as she realized she'd stepped in a lumpy pool of blood. The putrid smell of death and decay filled the air despite the breeze, and she nearly gagged.

The shifting of grass and a low snarl caught her attention. A Mooncursed corpse twitched and started to rise, all elongated, furry limbs and jagged fangs. The head of a wolf had been magically affixed to the dismembered bodies of several men with metal plates. Kassia froze, forcing herself not to scream or reach for the herbs to create a witchshield as the beast rose high above her head. She waited, knowing even the slightest movement would prompt an attack. It let out a mournful howl that broke her heart at its unending pain.

The poor creatures were victims in all of this. Her chest ached, as she knew what she had to do. Ever so slowly, she drew a potion out of her bag and readied to hurl it straight at its bone-plated chest.

Before she could, a fist-sized vine that ended in a lethal point drove through its throat, spurting blood forth in a fountain. It fell with a loud thud and didn't move again.

"Kassia?" Thaen asked.

Kassia blinked, eyes fighting to leave the gory sight to settle on the handsome naturalist warrior with long hair and dark skin. "Thaen, what are you doing here?"

"Demorra lit fires in the Seven Forests," Thaen said. "Once we pushed them back, I came to see if we could be of assistance to our allies. Are you all right?"

His deep brown eyes bored into hers, catching her up in the gaze. They'd met before, and even then, his contagious energy had been hard to stay away from. That'd been what felt like a lifetime ago, before Saryll had broken her heart. Thaen had always been handsome, but why couldn't she seem to peel her eyes away now?

When she didn't answer immediately, his warm hands came to rest on her arms as he checked her for injuries. "Did it hurt you?"

"No, no. I'm fine. I appreciate the help." She waved the potion vial. "I was about to cause a huge mess, so thank you."

He chuckled. "You were always handy with the witchy potions."

Kassia was about to reply when crunching grass interrupted. King Aradey—Theo—approached at the naturalist's side, cleaning his starlight blade before sheathing it at his back. She tore her gaze away from Thaen's to settle upon the blond once-blacksmith.

"Kassia, I'm glad you came," Theo said. "We can use all the help we can find. Let's get you to the tents. It's not safe out here."

"I'll join you," Thaen replied, flexing his hand to stretch the bark that had begun growing on his skin. "I can do more in the healer's tents than out here."

"Thanks." She stared at the slain Mooncursed.

Theo gestured for her to lead the way, and she forced her feet to move. The two men fell in line beside her.

Panning across the field, she asked, "Who survived?"

"Aurienne is in a coma but alive, thankfully," Theo replied. "The healers say that she will recover. Most of the others of our group survived. Saryll is also uninjured."

Kassia nearly stumbled again, relief flooding through her before the acrid taste of rejection drowned it. Saryll hadn't even thought she was worth giving their budding relationship a real shot. Kassia forced down the bitterness. It was for the best.

"Glad to hear it," Kassia said. "We haven't spoken, so I wasn't aware of the battle until I received your call."

Thaen glanced her direction, gauging her reaction as his gaze lingered, though she couldn't fathom why.

Theo paused before continuing, "Captain Laurier and Sentinel Kolten sustained minor injuries. Most of the forest giants went to slumber to protect the saplings. And the Wyndsel forces never showed up." He raked his hands through his matted, golden hair. "Thirty-three thousand, nine hundred, and eight Avyllonian soldiers are missing or dead. We'll have to take immediate steps to protect the Pillars to avoid this repeating."

The news seemed to pass right over Kassia. So many were dead. All the politics, battle tactics, and warfare were out of her realm of understanding. She clutched her protection charm as she took another look at the quiet battlefield.

Theo stopped outside of the tent. "Thank you again for coming. We really appreciate your help."

Nodding, Kassia stepped inside to find a sea of injured and dying. Setting down her bags, she and Thaen entered the fray.

"I'll follow your lead," he whispered. "Just tell me what to do."

"It's going to be a long day," she replied. "I'm just glad we're here to help."

Hours passed as Kassia focused on what she could—healing those left behind by the battles.

Charms & Potions

Chapter One

The forest protects those who remember its ways.

— *Wisdom of the Wildegrove Forest.*

1153 N.T.C. Wildegrove Forest. One month later.

Charms glowed faintly from baskets on the floor and bundles of drying herbs hung from ceiling beams as Kassia perched on a wooden chair beside a small counter to study her leather grimoire. Apothecary bottles, potions, and vials filled the bookshelves along with medicinal texts and wildecraft tomes. Athames, rolled up spell parchments, feathers, and a single human skull were tucked between the books and candles in the room. Kassia's dark hair hung in a single long braid down her back, twined with flowers and vines, and she pressed her palm into her curls as she read. Petals from the fresh blooms on her dress floated to the floor.

A small black cat leaped from the counter onto her back before stepping on her neck and head. Giggling, Kassia reached for it, finally catching it and pulling it against her chest.

"Hello, sweetheart. I would give you a name, but Grandmother always said that naming a cat was rude." She scratched it under the chin before rubbing its ears. "Is it rude?"

The cat nuzzled against her cheek.

Kassia glanced around the empty witch shop. "What should we do today?"

The cat purred as she scratched the white star on its chest for a moment before it jumped out of her arms and darted out the open window.

"I suppose I could harvest some lavendiir palm for tea," she said to herself. "With all the nightmares going around in the villages recently, we could use more."

Pursing her lips, Kassia stiffened at the thought of the magic-dampening, sleep-inducing tea. Not so long ago, she had offered it to the High Seer of Avyllon to keep her mind from bleeding out, without telling her how it would affect her gift. There had been a cost, and the seer rarely spoke to Kassia now, despite the fact that it'd saved her life. She shook away the gnawing sting at the lost friendship.

Kassia slid off her stool and out into the bright morning light of her garden to gather the tea. She followed the winding cobblestones through the lush garden beds, stopping to scratch the chin of one of the stray black cats meandering through the foliage.

The palms were nearly as tall as she was, hanging from a spiky-barked tree with misshapen purple fruit. She harvested three leaves and three of the weeping fruits and carried the armload past the door painted with bright floral designs and inside the cottage to the large wooden preparation counter. As Kassia began to scrape the prickly fuzz off the leaves, the cat with the star purred at her loudly. It had taken a liking to her and always seemed to be lingering nearby.

"What do you think is causing all of the night terrors?" she asked the cat. "And why is the forest so restless?"

The cat meowed in response.

Placing the scraping knife down, Kassia squeezed the fruit until it burst. She focused on catching the juices into the bowl, which created the aroma often described as purple rain—fruity, a little floral, fresh, and mild. After depositing the mixture into several glass jars, she corked and sealed them. She bundled the harvested leaves and hung them to dry from a beam in the ceiling.

Reaching through the open window, she plucked two purple flowers from a vine. She twined them into her braid, already feeling bursts of sparkly energy racing up her hair and sinking into her scalp. A cleansing breath centered her.

She was about to reach for another flower when the door burst open. A young man half-carried a woman with dark skin into the cottage. The woman's leg was bleeding and bent at an unnatural angle.

"Is there a healer here?" The man's voice cracked. "My wife fell and hurt her leg."

Kassia immediately gestured to a stout wooden chair beside the wall. "Yes, bring her here. What's your name?"

Sweat glistened off the woman's brow as she gritted her teeth. "I'm Mairwen. I was walking through the crop field and stepped into a rabbit hole, I think. I'm usually so careful—argh!"

Mairwen collapsed into the chair, her husband kneeling at her side to hold her hand as he glanced toward Kassia with a worried expression. A sharp pang caught under Kassia's ribs at the sight of his care for his wife. One day, she hoped someone would feel for her that way. Once, someone had, but it had ended quietly, as if it'd never happened. She swallowed the pain down as she hurried toward her medical supplies, collecting padding, splints, bandages, and the water always boiling in her small hearth pot. Returning to Mairwen, Kassia lightly felt down the bones, finding splotches of blood on her skirts.

"It seems you're lucky," Kassia said. "It's a clean break and should heal by the end of summer."

With a choked sigh, Mairwen leaned her head against the chair. "Thanks be to the gods."

Kassia dabbed a clean rag into the boiled water and shook it for a few moments to allow it to cool before cleaning the woman's leg. There were bruises and cuts, and she struggled to find the source until she cleaned the majority of the blood. As she did, she found bruises that formed four long lines of purple and blue with deep scratches.

The shape of a distorted hand.

Slowly, Kassia lifted her eyes to the woman's, searching for an explanation. The woman's eyes were wide with fear and pain. It wasn't the mark of a Mooncursed or a Shadow. Kassia shook her head, focusing on the task at hand.

It must be something else.

Taking a steadying breath, Kassia then reached for the padding, splint, and bandages. Images of the war-torn field flashed through her mind, and she gripped the edges of the splint until it dug into her palm. As she continued to position the materials, she tried to shake off the dark memories that wanted to devour her resolve.

You can do this. You've done this a hundred times.

Maybe that was a problem.

Kassia placed her hands onto the broken leg. "I'm sorry, Mairwen, but this is going to hurt. We must get the bones back into place so they can begin to heal."

Without warning, she applied pressure and counter pressure and snapped the bones back where they belonged.

Mairwen screamed, but Kassia was already wrapping it up with bandages and securing everything with a tight knot. She hated this part, but the relief that followed was a blessing.

"It's done," Kassia said. "I'm sorry for the surprise, but it's better if you can't tense up. It hurts less. And you're all set. Here are some extra bandages for when you need to rewrap it. You need to use a crutch and stay off the leg until after the midsummer Solariall festival. Come back to me in a few weeks so I can see how it's progressing or if the pain worsens."

The man helped his wife to stand, one hand under her arm and the other resting on the small of her back. Mairwen accepted a crutch from Kassia.

"Thank you," Mairwen said. "I don't know what we would've done without you. I can't believe I was so clumsy. I just thought I saw . . ." She shook her head. "Never mind, I must've been daydreaming. There have been rumors . . ."

Heart lurching, Kassia met the customer's fearful gaze. There had been all sorts of rumors rampant in the villages for months, but the current one was all too similar to the stories her grandmother had told her of the malefics. Malefic witches were evil magic users who twisted witches' magic into something sinister and bent nature to their will. The cost was great, turning them into corrupted hags with extra eyes and vines growing out of their skin. Kassia hungered for magic, but not if it corrupted all she held sacred.

Ancestors, gods, please protect us.

About to ask what the woman had heard, Kassia was interrupted by a dark blur outside the window. A cloaked woman stood at the tree line, unmoving, and then turned back into the woods and was gone. Unease and foreboding crept into Kassia's heart at the strange sight.

"Do you have any heartwood charms?" the woman asked. "My grandmother had one for many years and she swore that it was the best protection against malevolent magic. She said she purchased it here."

"I'm sorry. I've never heard of charms made from heartwood." Kassia's brow furrowed.

She knew every inch of the shop, every concoction, tonic, brew, and spell. Yet, she'd never heard of these. Vaguely, she recalled Miella, the last living kin of the vampires, wearing a necklace made of heartwood, but she wasn't aware of any protection properties. If there was—she should know about it as the future witch for the Wildegrove villages.

I'll have to ask Grandmother when she returns.

"Let me prepare you an elder rose protection charm, though," Kassia said.

Collecting a few items, Kassia began to meticulously knot the vetiver and weeping ivy into a tight bundle with elder rose buds. When it was done, she handed it to Mairwen.

"It's best not to venture out after dusk," Kassia said. "Remember, the forest protects those who remember its ways. The old wisdoms are more important now than they've ever been."

The front door swung open once more, and Kassia's grandmother, Lorayne, entered the cottage just as the man helped Mairwen limp out onto the cobblestone path through the garden beds. Lorayne smiled wide enough that the sides of her eyes creased as she tucked a flower into her long, gray braid.

"What did they need?" the older witch asked.

"Help setting a broken leg," Kassia replied.

"Ah. You've had quite a bit of practice at that."

Unfortunately.

Stepping toward the sink, Kassia scrubbed the dark skin of her hands with rose-scented soap as she tried to banish the haunting images of that battlefield far away. She scrubbed and scrubbed, seeing blood that wasn't there dripping between her fingers. Even darker images of the Mooncursed attack on the Avyllon caravan floated just beneath the surface of her memories, threatening to drown her.

Lorayne held out her hand, gesturing for Kassia to stop. Her palms were already red from the friction, and Kassia slowed her scrubbing. Sighing, she dried off her hands and looped arms with her grandmother as they exited the cottage.

"Are you all right?" Lorayne asked. "You've hardly spoken of it since you returned, but today must have brought up some painful memories."

Kassia looked toward the garden, finding solace in the swaying leaves. "More terrible than I'd imagined. There were so many injured."

Bones hadn't just been broken; they'd been shattered by behemoths. There'd been magical maladies, burns from sorcerers' alchemical brews, gouges and missing limbs from the Mooncursed. Everywhere, people had been screaming and dying.

Kassia blinked, coming back to the present as she said, "There were so many I couldn't save."

The Battle for the Flame Pillar had left the continent reeling. Tens of thousands had died in those bloody few miles, their bodies not even laid to rest.

"Unfortunately, when the battle is done, the survivors are often left to fend for themselves," Lorayne said. "At least Aurienne, Theo, and Rianne had the sense to tend to their people. Not all leaders do. Too often, the common folk are forgotten in the great wars. And while our leaders' sacrifices were great, we can't rely on them alone to protect us.

We're going to have to take matters into our own hands if we want all our people in small villages around the continent to survive."

Kassia's long braid brushed her back as she shook her head. "And Avyllon held back the empire for months before they took back the Pillar. If that was just the aftermath, I can't imagine what *they* saw, what's coming for us."

Her mind drifted to the cloaked figure standing at the tree line and the hand-shaped marks on Mairwen's leg. "I saw something on that woman's ankle. An injury not made by a natural creature or magic. It wasn't anything I've seen before."

"What do you think it is?"

Kassia reached for the small black cat rubbing against her arm. "There's something in the woods."

Hexes and Curses

Chapter Two

Nightflame and bloodrose curse,
Gods of the woods, hear my words,
To my enemy, do your worst.

— *Forgotten hex.*

Weeping ivy vines curled around Kassia's wrist. She couldn't help but smile as she stroked the velvet leaves that reached up to meet her touch. As she coaxed them around the trellis structure, they grew higher and higher before her eyes until they'd grown nearly five inches. Carefully, she untangled her hand from their knotted embrace.

"You're more active than you ought to be," she murmured to them, easing up on her stimulating energies.

The vines stilled, settling upon the smooth wood frame. Kassia stepped away from the raised box in her cozy garden. One day soon, this would all be her responsibility. Not just the gardens, but the nearby villages and all their needs. Kassia would take on the burden of caring for these people, allowing her grandmother a hard-won retirement.

Lorayne had promised the day was coming soon, which filled Kassia with excitement and apprehension.

She reached her hand over a parallel row of thymewrinkle, sensing the energy flowing between the plants through their interconnected roots. She pressed her palm into the damp soil, feeling the energy coursing through it as well.

"The land is waking," she whispered to herself. "What is causing you to stir?"

Kassia brushed the dirt from her fingertips, lost to her thoughts. Her grandmother had gone out to tend the garden that morning without so much as a word, leaving her feeling uneasy. Lorayne hadn't been the same ever since Kassia had told her about the unnatural injuries on Mairwen's ankle, and Kassia got the impression that the older woman was keeping secrets. She smiled to herself.

But what witch doesn't?

A strange wind trickled through the dark curls that had escaped her long braid, and she immediately stood, closing her eyes to listen to its secrets.

It whispered, "*Change is coming.*"

"What change?" she replied.

Each gust and flurry communicated in its own singsong voice, words only witches could hear.

"*Beware the tangled roots.*"

A chill washed over her spine despite the warm early summer sun. The wind knew something.

"Tell me," she coaxed.

"*There is darkness in the woods.*"

"Could you be more specific?" she asked.

Silence met her.

"Don't make me get my cards out," she chastised. "Secrets can't stay buried for long."

It was pointless to argue with the breeze, but today the strange feeling that wouldn't leave her alone left her stomach in knots. If the wind knew what was coming, it should save her.

The small black cat with a white star on its chest hopped up onto a stone wall beside her, mewing and arching its back until she ran her fingers through its silky fur.

"What do you think? Do the winds speak to you as well?" she asked absently.

The cat pushed into her, rolling its head against her hip before leaping into the thick leaves.

The air suddenly went deathly still as animals scurried away from her garden. A cloud drifted over the sun, casting a gray gloom across the meadow. Ravens cawed overhead, calling a warning to lurking danger. The cat bucked and hissed as it darted into the leaves.

Something is coming.

"Grandmother," Kassia called toward the back garden where her grandmother had been crushing seeds. "Come out here."

Chin to the sky, Lorayne stepped around the cottage, wielding a satchel of clinking potions. After the Mooncursed attacks, they'd prepared concoctions that would take down a lion.

Kneeling, Kassia felt for the energies of the roots beneath her feet. She ripped her hand back. They were all writhing in pain.

Anger flared in her throat. She could hardly believe what she suspected, but nothing else explained the twisted draw of power from her beloved forest.

"I'm going to help you," she whispered to the screaming plants.

A dark splotch of energy darkened the air just ahead.

She brushed off her hands, following the source of the intrusion toward a shadowy arch of trees just off the road.

Chills racing down her arms, Kassia braced herself as she approached the path into the woods. Keeping her grandmother behind her, she searched for the peril she knew must be lurking.

A cloaked woman stepped into a dark spot in the middle of the path, head down and palms open at her sides. She didn't move again, and even the wind seemed to pass around her.

Kassia's blood spiked with warning, and she stopped in her tracks. Her hand slipped to her neck until her fingers closed around the protection charm. She began to whisper a protection spell.

The woman's head slammed up, knocking her hood back. Kassia

choked on her breath as the woman's cloak slipped to the ground. Every muscle recoiled against her bones, as Kassia was unable to believe her own eyes. Dark olive twigs grew in and out of the witch's body, and extra eyes blinked from beneath the foliage on her arms that swarmed with roaches. Her expression was flat, almost dead, and the bones of her face seemed to shift under her skin.

Unable to think or speak, Kassia's limbs locked up at the sight of the fairy tale villain standing before her.

Malefic witch.

She didn't need to say it, as her grandmother was already holding up a handful of dangling protection charms in one hand, with an orange vial in the other.

"Go back where you came from, witch." Lorayne's voice was like claws on steel. "Or you won't leave this place."

Kassia scrambled for her own vials from her satchel, hands shaking so badly, she feared she might drop them. It was always like this before a battle. Adrenaline coursed through her, lending its strength to her blood.

"The power gathering here must be stopped," the malefic intoned, as if repeating the words of another.

The witch craned her head until something in her neck popped. A mouse crawled out of her mouth and scurried over her pale forehead and into her matted black hair. Recoiling, Kassia took another involuntary step back, every one of her instincts screaming at her to run.

"*Witches lurk these woods*" the wind whispered. "*Witches with the rotten blood of the betrayer.*"

Forcing her thoughts to focus, Kassia gripped her vials, preparing for the fight to come. Having fought Mooncursed in Avyllon, she knew what came next. She'd survived worse.

A rustling in a nearby leafy shrub drew the malefic witch's attention as the black cat with the star meandered onto the path. Fear speared Kassia in the chest at the sight of the small animal in danger. The witch's black eyes darted to the feline.

No.

Kassia didn't hesitate. The vial left her fingers and struck the witch on the side of the head. Orange fire exploded in branching swirls as the witch screamed and clawed at the cloudy flames licking her neck and ear.

With more strength than she ought to be able to muster at her age, Lorayne hurled her own vial toward the witch. The witch screamed again, and the small animals and insects skittered across her face and down her arm to avoid the flames.

Kneeling, Kassia pressed her hand to the dirt and whispered a prayer to the nature gods as she grounded herself. Feeling the vials in her hand warm and the glass start to shudder, she hurled them toward the witch.

With clawed hands outstretched, the malefic flew toward them, her mouth opening into a gaping maw that covered half her face. She darted right into the path of Kassia's shattering vials of corpseroot and nightrose. The shadows at the malefic's hands vanished as the potions dispelled the dark magic the witch had summoned.

Crooked, knotting vines speared out of the soil on either side of Kassia and Lorayne, and Kassia grabbed her grandmother by the arm to wrench her out of the way of their razor-sharp barbs. They both sprawled on the ground as they dodged the writhing shoots.

The witch stood over them, half her vine-bound face covered in charred, thrashing shadows as three more eyes opened, each bleeding thin green blood. She glanced between Loryane and Kassia as if deciding which she would claim. Snarling, she snatched Kassia's ankle and began to drag her off the path and into the trees. The malefic witch's icy talons dug into Kassia's flesh, leaving a ring of small punctures. The satchel slipped off Kassia's head as she was hauled away.

Screaming, Kassia clawed at the dirt, grabbing for roots and low-lying shrubbery branches as she kicked at her attacker's knees. Her fingernails chipped against the hard-packed ground and fallen tree limbs scratched her arms.

"Sisters! I have her," the malefic hissed to the trees.

The scent of honeysuckles filled her senses, and she whipped her head around. For a fleeting moment, she thought she saw a familiar face watching from the shadows. One she hadn't seen for years, but as quickly as she thought it appeared, it was gone. Vanished right before her eyes.

Mother?

Shaking off the strange feeling, she fought against the witch who only hissed in response as a roach ran across her nose. Kassia kicked her in the face, squishing the bug with a crunch. She kicked at the witch again, striking her in the neck with the heel of her boot. Kassia found a fallen branch and swung it at the witch, knocking her to the ground.

Lorayne rushed into the trees, slamming a glowing charm into the witch's temple.

Lorayne began to chant a hex, and Kassia joined her, clasping hands.

Bones of witches buried deep,
Secret winds, promises to keep,
Hear my words, protect your blood,
Hex the witch within this wood.

Tendrils of mud rose from the ground beneath the witch, pinning her in place. Kassia slipped a small, dark vial out of her pocket and grimaced at the malefic, waiting for the attack she knew would be coming. After striking such a blow, it would likely charge.

"Leave this place," Kassia told the witch, hoping that she would heed her words.

The malefic flew out of the trees with sharpened teeth gaping, magic weaving between her claws.

"We warned you," Kassia said before crushing the dark vial onto the witch's face.

Lorayne whispered a hex Kassia had never heard before against a pendant at her throat.

Nightflame hex and bloodrose curse,
Gods of the woods, hear my words,
To my enemy, do your worst.

An explosion of light nearly knocked Kassia back, and she covered her face with her arms. Blinking, she finally opened her eyes.

A charred blast mark was all that remained of the witch. The little black cat with the star pranced across the path, a furry, dead mouse in its mouth. It dropped its prey and licked its paw.

Kassia stared. "What happened?"

"The woods answered my call." Lorayne's eyes flashed with intensity. "It seems the rumors were true."

Malefic witch.

The stories, always changing, warned children to behave, to come in before dusk, to avoid the dark parts of the woods else a malefic witch would eat them. Yet, even with a child's wild imagination, she'd never pictured something as hideous as that woman. Even bloodwitches only sacrificed their own blood to increase the power of their works, but this sounded much worse. The heart of wildecraft was receiving what nature offered. Changing it, directing it, but honoring what was given.

"Malefic witches take from nature, corrupting the gifts and twisting the magic into something unrecognizable," Lorayne said. "And *these* witches have a darkness in them I've never sensed before. Oily and foreign and ancient."

The blood drained from Kassia's face. *Oily*? When she'd travelled to Avyllon, she'd heard only one type of magic ever described that way.

Kassia's voice was as small as possible, as if the very trees were leaning in to listen. "Emperor Rexil's dark goddess, Niamh, has magic like that. Do you think she could've used it to corrupt the witches?"

Lorayne inhaled. "Gods, help us all. We need to convene the Speakers of the Tangled Root."

Weeping Ivy

Chapter Three

Hexes, potions, witch's brew,
Curses none can undo.
Seeds rooting in the heart,
Magic twisting in the dark.

— *Poem scrawled in the corner of the Book of Wildecraft.*

Wrenching a weed out of her garden bed, Kassia reeled from the encounter with the malefic witch. Shaking her head, she watched the plants rustle as the small cat crept through the shadows cast by the sparkling sun. The cat stopped beside an old pair of trees that had twisted together at the top, forming an arch. As a child, Kassia had always made believe that it was a doorway to the fairy realm, and she'd spent hours braiding flower crowns under its shade.

Lorayne's silhouette finally came into view down the path, and Kassia watched as the older witch neared. Her grandmother set down a basket full of tied bundles of nightrose stems, thymewrinkle, and inferno flower. All ingredients for curses, hexes, or sorcerers' alchemical reactions—magics she'd tried to stay away from.

At Kassia's raised brows, Lorayne chuckled, her brown eyes dancing. "Whatever must be done. One day, I won't be here, and there are things you must know."

"I don't believe that for a moment. You're going to outlive us all." Kassia sat on the stone wall, allowing velvety leaves to brush against her forearms. "What aren't you telling me?"

"We haven't begun to see the extent of the Demorran magic, or the lengths they'll go to conquer the continent. You must prepare yourself to take drastic measures." Clasping her hands, her grandmother whispered a prayer to herself, chanting her protection rhymes three times over.

Kassia fingered a small stem crawling over the stone wall encircling the garden. She took a deep breath, preparing to ask her grandmother her questions head-on.

"What are the Speakers of the Tangled Root?" Kassia asked.

Lorayne glanced her direction, disapproval lingering in the slant of her brow. "You don't remember your lessons?"

Kassia smiled back, knowing her grandmother couldn't stay displeased with her. "I remember once you told me that they were a group of fairy queens as tall as my hand that flew through the trees fighting the evil forest nymphs for the crystals growing in the tree bark. I didn't suspect you were serious."

Lorayne's expression softened. "No, the tales of fairies doing battle in the trees was perhaps an exaggeration." She sighed. "In truth, it's a council of witches that only come together in times of great need to guide us. It's made up of the elder or most powerful witch from each region. Once the council has spoken, their will is carried out by the rest of the witches. Their ways are secret. They protect our ancient magics, sharing only with the Speaker and their protégé. I put out a call to them."

Blood prickling with icy anxiety, Kassia tried to shake away the images lurking in the shadows of her mind. The aftermath of the Flame

Pillar and Mooncursed attacks would haunt her for some time. The recent malefic only added to the darkness in her mind.

"Can the Speakers help the people?" Kassia asked.

"I believe so," her grandmother replied. "This time, you will join me."

Kassia took a steadying breath. "I will share what I witnessed at the Flame Pillar and before that, traveling the continent. Maybe it will help."

"We're lucky to have you." Lorayne patted her hand.

A raven landed on a nearby wall, hopping from stone to stone and cawing fearsomely before preening itself. A rolled-up paper was clutched in its claws.

"Tch," Lorayne said. "Thank you, dear."

First reaching up to caress the bird's feathers, she offered it a white stone from the garden before taking the paper. With a caw, it flapped its wings and flew off. Lorayne took a deep breath before breaking the seal and unrolling the message. She stared at it for a moment too long.

Concern flashed through Kassia's chest. "What is it?"

Lorayne looked up from the parchment, resolve flooding her eyes. "The Speakers answered the call. The council will convene. It's time I taught you the buried secrets of wildecraft. Dark magic has returned, and you'll need our most ancient spells."

Inferno flowers bloomed in the small back corner of the garden. Kassia hadn't realized how dangerous they were until she'd watched the orange vials ignite on the malefic's face. It wasn't until after that she realized why her grandmother had started growing so many. The black stems and leaves held the shimmering orange and yellow petals up to the bright sunlight. Careful not to touch the faint pulsing glow in the veins of the blooms with even the leather gloves she was wearing, Kassia inspected the small crop. It had taken years to get even this handful of seeds to thrive, but she now knew how potent each cutting could be.

"Remember," Lorayne said softly over her shoulder, "inferno

flowers are the blooms of the witches. They're one of the thirteen sacred florae of the forest."

The sacred florae were revered and incredibly rare. Nearly impossible to grow, the flowers only blossomed on energy-rich coils or lines in the forest network where the soil had been prepared with painstaking magic. Buried in the ground around them were iron charms, forest moss, and animal bones. They were tended to with water blessed by a full moon and fed with whispered blessings every day for a year, and then each flower only produced three seeds, many of which wouldn't take.

"I remember." Kassia knelt as she checked the black leaves for any signs of pests or underwatering.

Lorayne's tone turned serious. "Inferno flower mixed with the right charm and incantation will create a quick but hot explosion of flame. You need to whisper hexes as you gather, prepare, and reduce the liquid. It'll make it more potent, so we need fewer vials next time."

Freezing, Kassia glanced toward her sweet grandmother in disbelief. "That's a dark brew, Grandmother."

Lorayne waved her hand dismissively. "Power is power. All that changes is who the wielder is and what their intentions are. You must learn these things."

"I . . . uh—"

"Do you want to have a chance against the malefic witches?"

Kassia's expression hardened. As long as she didn't turn to bloodmagic or the malefic corruption of her wildecraft, she had to be willing to do anything. Even this. It was what was required of the witch of the region. She only wished she'd learned these techniques sooner. Suddenly, she began to think there were secrets she'd never uncover.

"You haven't been hiding all your best spells from me, have you?"

"Not on purpose," Lorayne said, and Kassia wasn't sure if she believed her. "I always hoped your mother would return to teach you these things."

Kassia pursed her lips with a dull ache in her heart. After her father had died all those years ago, her mother had vanished. Kassia had always wondered what happened to her. Her mother had loved her fiercely and wouldn't have stayed away unless forced. Perhaps those unanswered questions were why she had hallucinated her when the malefic attacked. The aroma of honeysuckles, her mother's favorite scent, caught her off-guard again, and she glanced toward the corner of the garden where she'd kept her mother's flowers.

Lorayne dabbed her eye before continuing. "There just hasn't been a reason before to focus on the more violent aspects of our craft. Your talents always were with healing and protection. Violence is the least important of what we can do. Our strengths are in healing and taking care of our people. Unfortunately, this side must still exist in times like these."

Suspicion floated in the back of Kassia's skull.

I didn't realize our magic could be used like this.

She chewed her lip. "When was the last time the council was called?"

"We meet every thirteen years or in an emergency. The last meeting was about eleven years ago, when you were a child. This one was called early to discuss the war."

Kassia remembered a few times when Lorayne had left for a few weeks when she'd been younger. She'd always assumed it was foraging and gathering. One of them must have been for the council.

"Inferno flowers and nightshade berries can create an acid explosion if you whisper an ancestral hex while mixing." Lorayne surveyed their garden with her wrinkled hands on her hips. "We don't have any more nightshade berries out here, and only a few remain inside. We'll have to see if we can find any on the way."

Her grandmother glanced toward the forest for the tenth time in as many minutes.

Kassia's brows pulled together as she sensed her grandmother's unease. "What aren't you telling me?"

Lorayne ignored her question. "There's one more brew you need to know. The most powerful of them all. Bloodrose, from those bloodwitches, heartwood, and inferno flower create a lethal, noxious cloud that burns your lungs from the inside out. It should only be used in the direst of circumstances."

Her grandmother leaned in to whisper the incantation.

Rivers, roots, earth, and sky,
Heed our call and rise up nigh.
With bleeding root and whispered fire,
Curse the foes and light the pyres.
Blessings on those who walk our path,
Our enemies shall turn to ash.

The words carved themselves into Kassia's memory at once. She never forgot an incantation.

Lorayne reached out to twist a small hellebore lily leaf that was peeking through a nearby window around her finger. "Remember that magic is all around you, if you know where to look. It's in the ground, the plants, people, everything. And we just gently nudge it in the direction we want."

Several large black cats ambled out of a rose bush, weaving between Lorayne's legs.

The older woman knelt, petting and scratching each before whispering, "I know. I will miss you, too. Be sure to visit often? I'll be waiting."

Kassia's brows drew together as she hurried to complete the tending, cutting, and weeding. "How long are we going to be gone?"

"About a week," Lorayne replied, hands slowing as the words left her mouth. "I can't tell you anymore until we arrive. We've been sworn to secrecy to protect each other and our magics."

How terrible will this council be?

Kassia swallowed, ignoring the urge to twist the end of her long braid, unable to shake the feeling of discontent. "Do you believe the war can be won, despite the High Seer's prophecy?"

"If the High Seer is going to succeed despite the musings of fate, she will need all the aid she can muster." Lorayne gave the cats a final scratch before pushing herself up to standing, her brown eyes warm. "We must do what we can to protect ourselves, or else we'll be washed away in the carnage."

"It seems impossible," Kassia said.

Lorayne brushed a rogue dark curl out of Kassia's face. "Small acts of courage make the impossible possible, but it will take all of us working together."

"*Unexpected allies spring forth,*" the wind whispered.

Lorayne tilted her chin up, listening as well. "It's time to go. Before we leave, let's make a few protection vials. It won't take long. I can show you how to work with inferno flower."

Kassia glanced around urgently, seeing so many tasks to finish. "Are you sure? I've never worked with it before."

"It's time. The flowers, bursting with the magic of the land, must be handled with care." Lorayne folded her hands. "Cut the stem just below the head of the bloom and be ready to collect the oil that will seep out."

Kassia lined up her shears where her grandmother had guided her, underneath the rolling black leaves and brilliant sunrise-colored flower head. Carefully, she positioned her basket underneath so the plant wouldn't inadvertently touch her skin. Then she cut, and the flower toppled down. With her other hand, she brought up the clear glass vial to the amber liquid oozing out of the stem.

"Good work," Lorayne continued. "Now pull the entire plant, root and all, and tip the remaining oil into the vial and cork it, quickly."

Breathing in the floral garden air, Kassia narrowed her gaze on the plant, following each of Lorayne's instructions to the word. It was incredibly potent. One could fuel dozens of brews and potions if handled correctly. And if mishandled, it would burn down the entire cottage and surrounding fields.

Lorayne leaned forward, watching intently. "Ever so carefully, place the stem and root into the basket and roll the flower face down on top of it. Wonderful!"

Kassia repeated the steps with the other flowers until her basket was full.

Done.

Kassia could finally breathe easier. Careful to keep her gloves away from Lorayne's skin, Kassia offered her grandmother her arm as they entered the cottage. Their skirts brushed the swaying grasses and wild poppies. The painted door closed behind them, and Kassia laid the basket with its fragile contents on the shop counter.

Lorayne trailed, looking over her shoulder. "Lay the flower face up on solid stone that has been washed with cleansing weeping ivy and Moonwater."

She waited until Kassia had completed the required cleansing, and Kassia was sure to doubly douse every inch of the surface. Any wildecraft interference could create an unwanted reaction or render the inferno flower unusable.

Once Kassia finished, Loryane continued the instruction, "Pry the seeds free and wrap them in gauze, healing moss poultice, Moonwater, and ash, then place them into a spelled box."

Using the point of her knife, Kassia freed the seeds and carefully wrapped them and set them into the protective spelled box. She would need to plant them soon, perhaps after they returned.

"Now slide your knife across the top of the petal, shaving off the glowing orange liquid," Lorayne said. "Place it into its own dark amber glass vial and cork it when you have completed all the petals. Use the pestle to grind the petals into a paste and place the paste in its own vial."

Kassia fell into a meditative state as she worked, her hands moving on their own as she followed Lorayne's instructions.

"Next, cut the stem from the root and chop it finely. Shave off the outer layer of the root and place it with the seeds, before cutting the roots into thin slices and adding them to the chopped stems and cork. The stem and roots you can eat in small quantities, but the rest is highly toxic."

I'm not sure I would ever eat any of it. It's too easy to mess up.

Hurrying to the sink, Kassia washed her hands with lavender lye in the warm water that had been simmering in the hearth.

"Now that it's done, we have what we need to create new potions," Lorayne said. "We may need them on our journey."

Apprehension slithered through Kassia's chest.

What happens at the Tangled Root?

Lorayne tugged the buckle of her satchel closed. "Pack your bags for an extra few days. We won't return until after the Speakers make their decision. And before that, there's one stop we must make along the way to prepare you."

Suspicion trickling down her spine, Kassia glanced up from where she was gathering her things. "What stop?"

"We must test your instincts to see if you're ready."

WITCH'S HEART

CHAPTER FOUR

The key to the woods lies in the witch's heart.

— *FOREST WISDOM.*

Frigid water eddied around Kassia's knees, chilling her skin to the bone. River rocks bumped against her ankles as she waded through the shallow current. Their mossy sheen threatened to toss her into the faster flows with each step. Small splashes soaked the bottoms of her knotted skirts. She'd been rock hunting for about half an hour and could no longer feel her toes.

"What does it look like again?" Kassia asked for the twenty-second time, beginning to doubt the stone existed at all.

"Clear quartz with a single white starburst in the middle surrounded by clouds," Lorayne called from the bank. "It'll be the only clear white stone you find."

Her grandmother's tone was the epitome of patience and kindness.

Kassia's teeth began to chatter, and each step sent spikes of pain up her legs. She wasn't going to be able to search much longer without warming up, but she needed to find the stone before they could leave for the witch council. A rock couldn't be what held her back from something as important as this.

"When are you going to look for yours?" Kassia called, dragging her hands through the crystalline water.

No reply.

Kassia looked up to see her grandmother doing her best to conceal a small smile. She stood and put her hands on her hips, realizing the answer.

"When did you find it?" Kassia asked.

"I don't need one," she replied. "And you'll find yours when you're meant to. It's less about the stone and more about your ability to find it."

Hag's teeth.

The numbness was spreading up her legs, signaling that it was time to get out. Kassia waded back to the shore and crawled up onto the bank beside the waiting fire. She plopped onto a folded blanket and began rubbing warmth back into her limbs.

She wanted to stuff her bare feet directly onto the coals but forced herself to maintain the distance required to keep her skin from blistering. The sharp prickling in her toes as the fire warmed her blood nearly made her reconsider. She hissed through her teeth.

"Why do we need the stones?" Kassia asked.

Lorayne smiled, adjusting her long, leafy skirts. "It's an offering to the Grove of the Tangled Root. Every council, the new attendees who will one day take over as Speakers bring cloudstar quartz and add their stone to the spiral. It's a connection to all the witches of the past. And it helps you find your way."

"And if I can't find one?" Kassia groaned.

"You will." Lorayne placed heated stones into the soles of Kassia's boots before settling back against a crooked tree. "When you're meant to."

"Why didn't you tell me any of this?"

"You were too young." Lorayne rolled her quartz between her fingers. "We do not tell our young witches until they are old enough to take the vows to keep our secrets. People have not always been so accepting of us."

Kassia's heart pounded. "What secrets?"

Lorayne smiled. "Our true power. I've already shared the witchshield with you, and some powerful curses and remedies. But there is much more to learn. These are the things we keep hidden. People are comfortable with witch healers who gather herbs to mend their loved ones, who worship nature in revelries, but sometimes when they see what we can really do, they make grave errors. These abilities are the ones that are not to be shared. Only witches who can be trusted to use them justly are permitted to learn."

Kassia leaned back, her hands pressing into the fallen leaves as she breathed in the forest deeply. Her blood raced with excitement, despite the dire circumstances. She could almost feel the power thrumming in the tree roots.

Her finger brushed against something cool and hard. Turning, she picked the object out of the dirt and grass. A small white stone, perfectly oval, with a white cloudy starburst in the center. Grinning, she held it up toward her grandmother.

Cloudstar quartz.

"You trusted your intuition." Loryane grinned. "I told you it would find you when you were ready. We'd better break camp. We have a ways to go before you meet the Speakers of the Tangled Root."

Heartseed Rite

Chapter Five

The heart of a witch's power comes from nature, not within herself. Bloodmagic corrupts the gift of nature and is forbidden.

— *The Law of the Tangled Root.*

Gnarled, woody vines branched across the forest floor in a woven tapestry of browns and reds around Kassia. The path through the woods curved among the trees and over the hills, leading toward the hidden grove before splitting in every direction. Kassia wondered how anyone avoided traveling in circles.

As if reading her mind, her grandmother answered, "Use your cloudstar quartz. Reflect the sun's or moon's light off the stone and toward the path. The correct one will light up. Once you've been there, you won't need to do this again. The shielding spell will lift for you."

Kassia lifted her stone to catch the spots of sunlight dotting the air and guided the little spot of light across the path until crushed small white pebbles shimmered.

"There's crushed cloudstar quartz in the dirt?"

"This entire wood is hexed and magicked by generations of witches to protect against intruders. None that weren't invited can unravel the mysteries of this place," Lorayne replied, her voice trailing off. "But any secrets remaining are hidden in my grimoire."

Kassia lifted her head. "And where is that?"

"Hidden in the woods behind a locked door without a key."

Shaking her head, Kassia continued using her quartz to illuminate the correct path. She stepped over the stout, pulsing vines as she followed her grandmother deep into the heart of the sacred forest north of Wildegrove. A chilly breeze, far too cold for early summer, filtered through the thick canopy, and she pulled her wool cloak around her shoulders. Though it was only mid-afternoon, the dense foliage now blocked out the sun, and they'd had to light torches several hours ago. They must be close, as Kassia glimpsed several other torches in the distance moving in the same direction.

"We're here," Lorayne murmured.

The air crackled with energy as Kassia stepped into a small grove of crimson-barked heartwood trees. A large spiral of cloudstar quartz pebbles swirled between the pulsing vines and fallen scarlet leaves. One by one, witches knelt to place their stones at the end of the spiral pattern. Kassia followed Lorayne and placed hers between the others, feeling the steam arising from the newest stones.

Kassia studied the grove. At the center, a heartwood tree towered high over the canopies of the surrounding, smaller heartwoods. She noticed that it had been carved or grown to resemble a woman, tall enough that the lofty branches became her hair. Leaning sideways, Kassia then realized that each side of the tree had been shaped like a different woman. With this size of tree, there were at least six depictions, covered in vines, ferns, and snails.

Standing, she noticed large, flat, rune-carved boulders placed before each of the thirteen heartwood trees, and elderly women sitting upon several of them. She glanced toward her grandmother.

"Speakers sit upon the stones," Lorayne whispered, sitting on the nearest one. "The rest of the witches stand between the trees and to the outside of the circle. You'll learn the secrets once you've sworn the unbreakable oaths on a heartwood tree."

Kassia stood to the side of her grandmother as a foreboding weight descended upon her shoulders. Something about this wasn't adding up. The energy of the grove crackled, yet there was a somberness in each of the Speakers she'd only seen once before: with Mathis before he'd made the ultimate sacrifice.

Why all the secrets?

As more witches arrived, fireflies floated out of the ferns. Across the glade, a stag and doe crept through the grasses, stopping to view their conclave before moving on. Kassia glanced around at the others, a collection of women from every corner of the continent, united by their apparent love of nature: clothing woven from ferns and grasses, flowers wound into their hair, medicinal bags at their hips, and fingertips stained from gathering.

The final elder witch sat upon her boulder and crossed her tan legs under her woven-reed skirts. "I am Speaker Persicaria. All Speakers are present, so the time has come to begin this coven meeting. We have called this gathering out of cycle to discuss the Darkling War upon us."

"But first, the oaths for our new witches," another said. "As nature embraces you, will you embrace the ways of nature?"

"Yes," the young witches all answered. Kassia was the slowest to speak as her mind mulled over the information.

The air was heavy. These words held meaning. Ancient oaths such as these were not broken lightly.

"Will you keep the secrets of your ancestors and of this council?"

"Yes."

A pop of power crackled through the grove. The oaths were set by powerful and ancient magic that Kassia didn't fully understand. The heartwood trees loomed over them, as if hearing their words.

"Will you turn from corrupted magic and remain steadfast to the gifts of the land?"

"Yes."

"Will you do all in your power to protect your fellow witches and humans?"

"Yes."

"Then welcome to the Coven of the Tangled Root."

Kassia took a deep breath as a weight settled upon her. The golden-threaded oaths were a tangible thing, connecting the Speakers with the new initiates, stretching across the forest toward other witches across the continent. The sparkling threads faded as they sank deep into the bedrock.

Lorayne said, "A heartseed rite has been called."

The eldest witches around the circle exchanged grave looks, while the younger counterparts blinked in confusion. A raven crowed from the canopy, and Kassia glanced upwards to notice dozens of the birds watching on. The unnatural sight brought chills to her skin, and she crossed her arms tightly.

A Speaker wearing layers of seashells said, "So soon? Surely, we have time."

A pale-skinned Speaker across the circle said, "A meeting has been called by Speaker Lorayne. A malefic witch attacked Wildegrove. We have all felt the corruption of the Shadows draining our magics as they fight their way into our land. It will only get worse. The Darkling Prophecy foretells destruction, and we, too, have seen it in the readings of our cards and the whispers of nature. The call asked us to decide whether it is time for a heartseed rite."

"Speaker Solveig is correct," another Speaker said. "If we wait to act, we will be too late."

Speaker Solveig retorted, "We all know what it means, but there may not be a way. The birth prophecy for the High Seer states we are all but doomed. She is our destruction or salvation, and it's not been decided yet. Until then, we must do what we can."

"There is nothing left to do. Malefics always work in covens," Lorayne added. "We found one, but there will be others. It took many vials and hexes as well as a blessing of the forest and us working together to finally defeat the malefic. If there had been two or three? We wouldn't be alive."

"How do you know it was a malefic witch and not a bloodwitch?" Speaker Solveig asked.

"There is no mistaking a malefic," Lorayne announced. "The blinking eyes peering out from underneath layers of vines growing out of the skin, as well as the oozing green blood and pitch-black eyes. It's as if the witch was plucked from our stories."

The Speakers exchanged worried glances, whispering to one another in hushed tones.

"Our time is up." Lorayne said. "Something far worse than the foreign emperor realizes trails his efforts, and that's where true destruction waits. He has no understanding of the deals he's made. The ancient blight returns, and none will be safe. The very land wakes to protect itself, to protect us. This is the fight for the future of the continent. We may already be too late."

Another Speaker said, "We have the protections of the elemental magics of old."

Lorayne argued, "This is our chance to keep the Shadows, and worse, out of the continent. Their presence here weakens the heart of the land. Their magic is not meant to exist here."

Speaker Persicaria shook her head, beads clacking in her curly hair. "The Mooncursed beasts drive deeper and deeper into the continent, and we have been informed by the High Seer that they're searching for a way to allow the Shadows in. They could find it any day, unfortunately."

Lorayne said, "This council was assembled for a reason all those years ago. This has been our purpose. I will answer this calling."

Kassia struggled to keep her face neutral. What were they talking about? Rites and ancient duties? Were these the secrets that her grandmother had been speaking of? What did it all mean?

The Speakers were quiet.

"I call for a vote to undertake the heartseed rite." Lorayne's voice cracked the grove like lightning against stone.

The Speakers exchanged somber gazes.

"The rite has been called," Speaker Solveig announced. "A unanimous vote is required. Raise your hand if you agree to the heartseed rite."

Lorayne's hand was the first to rise. More slowly extended upward. One Speaker shook her head and stepped down from the boulder. A grimacing younger witch with tension threading her shoulders took the other's place and raised her hand. All thirteen Speakers voted yes.

Lorayne reached for Kassia's hand and gave it a firm squeeze. "We will stay here and offer our strength until the threat is done. Do not be afraid of what comes, dear."

Kassia *was* afraid, as all of her senses were screaming. Even the wind rustled anxiously. What was happening? What weren't they telling the new initiates, and why did the Speakers look as though they were heading to battle?

"We begin by cleansing the grove," Speaker Persicaria announced.

Witches drew smudging bunches from their packs and lit them in the torches. All colors of smoke surrounded them.

Speaker Solveig turned to the newly initiated. "Witches, take the heartwood heartseeds you will be offered. Plant them throughout the continent. Use all your skills and magic to summon the trees and make charms for all you can."

A dark and heavy weight spread through the air as the Speakers spoke as one. "The Speakers of the Tangled Root offer our strength to the land. We honor the ancient pacts."

A vine detached from each of the thick heartwood trees behind each Speaker. They slithered through the air toward the center of the cloudstar quartz spiral. The end of each was a long, pointed tip. They grew and grew as the Speakers chanted. The vine behind Lorayne's tree wound its way beside Kassia's ear, and a sinking sensation blossomed in her stomach.

"As our ancestors before us and our descendants after us, we form an unbroken chain through history," they chanted. "We are born, we live, we die and return to the land to be reborn. Our magic connects us. The land protects us. We offer this sacrifice so the cycle may continue."

Sacrifice?

Kassia's chest constricted. The hazy air, the torches, the chanting, the somber expressions. The reaching vines had slowed, turning those deadly points back out to the circle. She took a step backward.

"I offer my heart," they finished.

The realization hit too late. "No!" Kassia cried.

The vines shot forward, striking each Speaker in the chest and impaling them against the tree behind them.

Kassia lurched forward to Lorayne's side. The vine was embedded in her heart, and smaller vines already spread through her chest. Dark brownish-red sap oozed out of the gaping wound.

"No, no, no," Kassia sobbed.

Shock coursed through her, and she felt as though all the blood drained from her hands and face. Every breath was a struggle as tears soaked her cloak. Her grandmother, kind and caring, always willing to help, had just been brutally injured—and had brought it upon herself. Her brain hurt, her heart hurt, even her soul ached.

"Why did you do this?" Kassia demanded as sobs wracked her body. "I could have taken your place!"

"This was my duty," her grandmother whispered, blood dripping from her mouth. "Yours is to spread the protection we offer. Now promise me."

Kassia had no idea how to do what had been asked of her, but she found herself saying, "I promise."

Tears streamed down Kassia's face as she hovered her hands beside the seeping wound, wanting to heal it but knowing she couldn't.

Wincing, Lorayne reached into the wound, digging past the protruding vine, and plucked a single crimson seed the size of an acorn. "Take this heartseed. Plant it where it is needed," Lorayne wheezed.

Kassia accepted the gift and stared at it numbly. Across the glade, the thirteen Speakers offered seeds to their newly sworn successors.

With a tight grimace and weak hand, Lorayne reached deeper inside of the gaping wound, plucking another seed, twice the size of the other that seemed to pulse with a soft inner light.

"And this one, it is the key to everything. Take the sap and harden it by the fire. It is"— Lorayne wheezed—"protection. Promise me you'll keep it safe. You'll know where to plant it, just listen to your heart."

Her grandmother stilled, and Kassia knew she was gone. Kassia swallowed another sob and collected a small vial of the heartsap. She pressed the cork into it, feeling as though her mind were detaching from reality. It was too awful, too nightmarish.

This can't be happening.

Rustling of branches caught Kassia's attention, and she noticed that the tree canopies all began to grow inward. Branches were connecting and knotting. The grove was sealing itself shut.

Saplings leaned in, filling the gaps between the trees. Vines grew from the forest floor, leaving only a single exit.

"I won't let you down," Kassia whispered.

The new council of witches, armed with the gift of the elders, exited the grove just as the final gaps closed.

Kassia cradled her sap-soaked heartwood seeds with shaking hands.

Her grandmother's voice quietly echoed in the wind. "*The land will rise up to defend those who hold its blessing.*"

Forlorn Paths

Chapter Six

The forest is full of lonely paths.

— *Forest wisdom.*

Kassia's tears had long dried as she mindlessly followed the path back to Wildegrove. Salt flaked off her cheeks as she clutched the heartseed to her chest. The other surviving witches, now the future Speakers taking the places of their kin and mentors, followed her in a silent crowd. Their homes were spread across the continent, but perhaps they also felt the sharp pain of loneliness that sat just beneath her breastbone.

Maybe they're seeking a few moments together before we all must uphold our promises to the ones who left us.

Wordlessly, the witches dispersed into the village as she followed the road back to the cottage. They would know where to find her. If she focused, she could feel the connection between each Speaker, pulsing with each heartbeat. But before she took up her duties, she had a few tasks to accomplish first.

Another tear slipped out, blazing a new trail in the lines streaking her face. Was that anger taking hold inside of her? She had no right to be upset with her grandmother for sacrificing herself to give them a chance. Yet, she couldn't help it.

How could you leave me alone?

How could you not warn me?

Balling her fists, she clenched her jaw until it throbbed. Passing through the garden, she blinked back stinging tears, as it all had no right to be as colorful as it was. Not with how empty she felt. Numb, she pushed open the door but lingered on the doorstep. If she half-closed her eyes, she could still see the swish of her grandmother's skirts drifting across the floor as she prepared another brew or potion. She could smell the scent of lilies that followed Lorayne everywhere she went. But when she opened her eyes, reality came crashing back.

The cottage was the same as she'd left it, but somehow, it no longer felt like home. The hearth was cold. No cats could be seen anywhere. Even the skies seemed dull. Her grandmother had been the heart of this home. Without her, it was just another place without a soul.

After her father had died in a wildfire and her mother had disappeared right afterward, she'd been left with her only remaining kin, Lorayne. Growing up, she'd only known never-ending love and encouragement from her grandmother, but now she was gone. New tears streamed down her face as she pressed her palm against her breastbone to try and lessen the deep ache burrowing into her chest. Nothing would bring her grandmother back, and yet she had to complete the rite as if the only person in the world who loved her wasn't gone.

The weight of it all threatened to crush her. She had to stand alone in the world, facing the darkest of witches, without anyone beside her. And apparently, she had never learned the secrets she was meant to when she took over the position. She was woefully unprepared, alone, and unwilling to accept failure.

Pushing back from the stool, she found a small jar of funeral seeds. Her chest was tight, and she found it hard to breathe, but she had to remember her grandmother properly and complete the memorial ritual. This was the tradition of the witches. She ambled out into the garden, finding a sunny place between the sky-blue forget-me-nots and the white elder rose. Breathing in, she smelled the nearby honeysuckles.

Her grandmother's true grave may be miles away, but this was the place that Kassia would remember her. Teary eyes implored the skies above.

What do we do with all the heartseeds?

What is the key?

How can I defeat malefic witches?

Lowering her eyes, she began to dig. The world was comforting under her fingertips, siphoning the smallest measure of her pain as it grounded her to the energy of nature. Wiping the tears again and smearing dirt on her face, she dropped a handful of hellebore lily seeds inside. The white oval seeds landed in the hole, and she covered them back up with a blanket of soil. Her sorrow watered the plot as she knelt in the garden, knowing when she stood, she would no longer be afforded the opportunity to grieve. Too much was at stake.

Kassia could sense the beating of twelve witch hearts approaching in the roots beneath her fingers. Brushing the dirt off her hands, she stood to find the other witches, the new Speakers, gathering just outside her cottage wall. Each clutching the precious seed they'd been given, they looked to one another for guidance. They hadn't been prepared any more than she had.

Their eyes asked the questions that their mouths did not. *What do we do?*

She wanted to scream that she didn't and might never know. The council had taken the wrong witch. Lorayne should be here. But her grandmother had trusted her. She'd always wanted to become the foremost witch of the Wildegrove, and stepping forward in hopeless situations like this was what that role required.

Instead, she took a deep breath and said, "There is much we don't know, but they gave us a directive. We must plant the heartseeds to create the protective shield. Once the trees are strong enough, we'll begin to create heartwood protection charms for our people that will ward off malevolent magics."

"Won't that take years?" a witch with bright red hair that Kassia didn't recognize asked.

"Not if we tend them," Kassia answered. "The Speakers wouldn't have given us a task that we can't complete. There will be a way. We just have to find it."

An idea struck, the faintest hint of a plan, if it could even be called that. Kassia hurried inside the cottage and went to the bookshelf, running her fingers across the aged spines of the tomes. Stopping when she found it, she opened the book and ripped out a page.

Returning outside, she placed the map on the side of a stone wall. "Everyone mark where you're from. We'll have a general idea where we will plant the heartseeds and can find one another if we need. Maybe it'll tell us where I need to plant the key."

"We just go home?" one witch asked.

Kassia's hand moved to the seeds around her neck. "The heartseeds need to be tended to, protected. They are all we have, so we can't afford to leave them alone. It will be a sacrifice, but we must do our small part in all of this."

The witches took turns marking the map with smudges of berry juice or flower petals until it was complete. Kassia leaned forward to study it, seeing that there was one section of the map that had no seeds—the Seven Forests.

Sending a prayer into the trees, she returned inside to search for parchment and an inkpot to write a letter to the sorcerer, Adonis. After she mourned, she knew she had to plant one of the seeds on the other side of the continent, where there were no witches, if she wanted the protections to extend that far. She didn't know the locations of all the Ways, but if Adonis could help portal her through to the Seven Forests, it would save her significant time—especially when she wanted to first assist the others with their tasks to ensure her grandmother didn't die in vain.

Hesitating, she scribbled a quick line informing Adonis and his sister, the High Seer, about Lorayne. It was best they knew the broad strokes of what had happened there. She finished the letter and sealed it with a dab of protection-spelled wax.

Kassia clicked her tongue, holding up the letter and a handful of nuts, seeds, carrots, and a shiny blue rock. She waited a few minutes before clicking her tongue again. On the third time, a raven flew through the open window and landed on her hand, picking at her offerings. She slid the letter into its claws and stroked the back of its head as it gobbled up the food.

"Adonis Azarrah in Avyllon," she whispered.

With a caw, it snatched the rock and darted out the window. Whispering a prayer to the forest gods, Kassia returned outside to the waiting group.

Kassia squeezed her skirts. "One last thing, we should go in pairs or groups to avoid the malefic witches in the woods."

The other witches exchanged worried glances.

"When my"—she swallowed a sob—"my grandmother and I encountered it, they were even more horrible than the stories ever said. We must stand together and, above all, be prepared. Take charms, hexes, spells, potions, curses, whatever you have."

And even then, it won't be enough.

First Roots

Chapter Seven

The heart of the forest beats with the blood of witches.

— *Grimoire of the Wildegrove witch, Lorayne Guara.*

Thirteen witches paired off in groups of three or four to plant the precious seeds. They'd hardly had the chance to learn each other's names before they scattered to the corners of the continent. Kassia waited in the garden with the three remaining witches of her group.

She had met Gwinifer a handful of times before, as she lived in one of the villages just outside the Wildegrove. Gwinifer's skin was as black as her hair, and her eyes were a molten brown.

The other two, she'd never met. Wrenn sat on the garden wall, spreading her embroidered crimson skirts on the stones. Strangely, she had one brown eye and one gold, and a fluffy orange cat followed her everywhere she went. Her skin was a medium brown, slightly lighter than Kassia's own skin, and her wavy hair was almost black. She'd hardly said a word beyond her name.

Delphia, on the other hand, hadn't stopped chattering, filling the somber air—as though her thoughts would fill the empty space in her heart.

"Do you think the heartseed is safe in a leather pouch pendant?" Delphia asked no one in particular. "Should I keep it in my satchel? Goddess—my aunt would know. Are we supposed to keep it dry? Or will it dry out like a bean? What are you all doing with yours? Is there a deadline to get it planted? What if it dies?"

Twirling her fire-red hair, the witch rubbed at the freckles under her puffy eyes. She paced the garden, stopping to sit before standing again to pace.

Kassia opened her mouth to answer any of the dozen questions that Delphia had posed but couldn't find an opening.

"What if my seed dies and my aunt died for nothing?" Delphia's voice was rising.

Wrenn caught Delphia's hand on the way by and gently pulled her to sit beside her on the mossy, low wall.

"You must remember to breathe." Wrenn's quiet, unmistakable strength filled the garden. "Wildecraft is about opening your mind to your instincts and what nature desires to tell you. Can you listen to the wind?"

"No." Delphia's foot bounced against the path.

Wrenn smiled gently, squeezing firmly on the redhead's knee to still the nervous energy. "How does nature speak to you?"

"I hear singing in the bones of my ancestors," Delphia replied.

"Try to listen to it now," Wrenn encouraged. "The answers are there."

Delphia gripped a finger bone pendant around her neck, closed her eyes, and began to chant softly.

"Gwinifer is from just outside of Wildegrove," Kassia cut in, trying to refocus the group on their task. "We should plant her seed first. Oakwood is the next closest, then Heartspring is just across the valley. I hope that we're all meant to plant it close to home. It's at least a place to start."

Kassia picked at her fingernails, feeling nervous energy coursing through her veins as well, just below the heavy grief. The small black cat rubbed against her leg before wandering over to sit several paces away from Wrenn's orange one. Kassia exhaled a long breath. Wrenn was right. Before they began their journeys, they all needed to be in the right mind and at peace, else they might miss the cues of nature.

"Perhaps we should do a cleansing ritual before we leave?" Kassia asked, holding out her hands to the others.

Wrenn slipped off the wall and took one hand while Gwinifer accepted the other. Delphia allowed her bone pendant to fall back against her neck as she completed the circle. As soon as Delphia touched Wrenn and Gwinifer, a crackle of energy raced through them and the winds above gusted. All four witches inhaled the sharp, biting air at the same time. Sounds intensified, and Kassia could hear the footfall of a deer a mile away, the tweeting of baby birds in the trees beyond the village, and the bubbling of a faraway stream. The ground seemed to root them in place, and Kassia couldn't have moved her boots if she tried.

Wrenn's palm was warm against Kassia's, like a blazing fire on the other side of a stone hearth. Burning inside but subtle on the outside. A reflection of the witch's magic, Kassia realized. On the other side, Gwinifer's touch was cool, like the popping bubbles atop a refreshingly chilly stream. It ebbed and flowed with the wind and her heartbeat. Through the chain, Delphia's energy was the static before lightning or the popping of a too-hot fire. Kassia could sense her own magic as well, all twirling vines and tendrils that grew between stones. The energies speared down into the roots below, connecting them to the magic of wildecraft.

Then she sensed their fear and the same questions in their mind that she now asked. Their doubts. Hopes. And then came the grief they all shared at losing a mentor or kin. The emotions raced around the circle, and suddenly, she knew these three women better than she'd ever known anyone.

Instantly, Kassia knew Gwinifer had fallen in love with a green-eyed girl from Wyndsel and used to sneak out to meet her beside the sea. When no one was looking, the witch would slip her head beneath the surface of the river and watch as the fish made homes of the rocks and grasses below. Delphia, on the other hand, loved kissing boys and leaving them fawning after her. She'd lit her village's annual bonfire from the time she'd been two years old with crushed herbs that even her aunt couldn't identify. She also was handy with a dagger and longbow. And Wrenn dug crystals out of the soil with her bare hands to line every shelf, window, and door of her cottage. She never spoke a harsh word but wouldn't hesitate to level a dark hex upon any who wished harm upon another. Kassia knew all that, and yet the circle showed her none of their wildecraft—instead keeping more layers of secrets.

Their magics flowed into one another, and Kassia instinctively knew any spell uttered while connected to the others would be unimaginably powerful. She couldn't fathom the power that would come from completing the heartseed ritual. Kassia began to pray, and the ground released its hold on her.

Spirits, gods, fallen blood,
Bless this path through the wood.
Bark, river, cloud, and stone,
Guide our path and bless our home.

The other witches joined in, whispering her words as they began to turn counterclockwise in a slow circle. Each repetition gained speed, leaving Kassia's skin prickling, until the seventh turn. A starburst of energy exploded from their clasped palms, radiating waves of green light into the skies. Kassia felt a shimmering blanket of protection settle upon them, and it was as if the eyes of the trees were now watching.

Glancing at one another, the witches released hands, and the energy finally faded.

Wildegrove's sprawling forests extended for miles in every direction. Kassia, Wrenn, and Delphia quietly followed Gwinifer. A full day and night had passed as they'd wandered. They'd long abandoned the roads, instead following narrow game trails through the trees, hills, and streams. Yet, Kassia never worried about getting lost. The trees hummed and the breeze whispered, and even the very soil beneath her feet guided her every step.

Eyes half-lidded, Gwinifer clutched her seed to her chest and led them deeper and deeper into the woods until even the sun hardly peeked through the canopy to observe their progress.

"Do you feel anything?" Delphia whispered.

"There's *something*, like warm lines running beneath our feet," Gwinifer said. "I think it's leading this way."

She paused abruptly, stilling as she quietly swayed in the wind—as if it were whispering secrets to only her.

"Here," Gwinifer said.

"Are you sure?" Kassia asked.

Gwinifer smiled at the protected grove and small bubbling stream, eyes sparkling. "It's here."

Kassia's own two seeds, safely tucked into a small bag around her neck, were silent, dormant. It seemed unlikely that both were meant to protect the Wildegrove.

How long must I travel before I know where to plant mine? And what do I do with the key seed?

Gwinifer knelt several paces away from the stream and scooped up handfuls of dirt before pressing her own heartseed into the hole. Then she covered up the seed, burying it deep into the heart of their wood before emptying a flask of Moonwater onto it.

Gwinifer looked up to Kassia. "What do we do now?"

I wish Grandmother were here. She would know.

Her heart ached at her grandmother's absence. Most days, Kassia still couldn't believe she was truly gone. More than once, she'd turned to the sound of an opening door or the scent of lilies, expecting to find her grandmother there, before harsh reality shook her to the core. Even on her journey with the Avyllon caravan, she'd always known where her home was and that it would be waiting for her when she returned. Now, homesickness and grief overwhelmed her. Her parents had already passed on or vanished, so with her grandmother gone, she was truly alone.

What do we do now?

The only thing we can do.

"We help it to awaken and grow," Kassia finally replied.

Nodding, Gwinifer crossed her legs and sat in the dirt beside the tree, pressing her fingertips into the soil. Kassia joined her, seeking the currents of magic running through the root systems beneath the ground and guiding it toward the precious seed. Allowing herself to fall into a deep meditation, she remained still for hours as she encouraged the little seed to drink in the magic.

Wildecraft, as her grandmother had always told her, wasn't naturalist magic. It was a question, not a demand. Coaxing. Far away, a small tendril of magic stemming from the Tangle Root grove reached for the heartseed, and she wove patterns to strengthen the connection.

Days and nights passed in deep meditation, with the witches only taking quick breaks for water or food. At some point, rain began to fall, and Kassia tilted her head back so it would soak into her skin. Her magic was soft, subtle, but eventually she sensed the little seed crack open with a shudder and a small sproutling begun to burrow up through the dirt.

Kassia and the other two witches stood, leaving Gwinifer sitting beside her seed.

Breathing in the magic of the air, Kassia said, "Take care of this as if your life depends on it."

All our lives do.

OAKWOOD

CHAPTER EIGHT

Forest spirits may take the form of an animal when they so choose to become a companion to a witch.

— *GRIMOIRE OF THE WILDEGROVE WITCH, ISENARA, 673 N.T.C.*

The Oakwood's mountains rose to the northeast as Kassia and her companions reached the rolling foothills and sparse trees. The villages were still about ten miles to the west, but they hadn't wanted to veer too close in an attempt to avoid attention.

"*There are witches in the woods,*" the wind whispered.

Kassia froze, tilting her head as the warning passed by. Wrenn glanced in her direction to share a knowing look.

"We need to hide now," Kassia said. "There is a malefic nearby. We should cast a witchshield."

"There's a stream just over there with a little protected clearing." Wrenn looked up toward the waning sun. "We can camp there for the night."

With worried glances cast in all directions, the trio hurried through the grass and the pine trees. The birds stopped their song just as they arrived.

"*Witches, witches, witches,*" the wind whispered.

Kneeling, Kassia dragged her hand through the dirt to create a circular trough surrounding them, trying to ignore the sickly sweet smell emanating from the other side—like rotten honeysuckles. Wrenn followed, dropping tiny crystals at measured intervals. Kassia began sprinkling vetiver root and red salt in the channel while Delphia added white dust from a small leather pouch. Striking a match, Kassia began whispering her prayers as she lit the circle on fire. She joined hands with Wrenn and Delphia, chanting the words over and over as the fire raced around them. The witchshield snapped into place with an audible pop.

"*Don't breathe,*" the wind whispered. "*She can smell your fear.*"

A cloaked malefic witch prowled by with knees bent a little too severely as she crept through the forest.

Delphia bit her fist to silence a scream as Wrenn paled. Kassia squeezed Delphia and Wrenn's hands and clung to them silently, sending comfort through the touch. She didn't dare reach for her satchel of vials. The witchshield was supposed to cover sounds as well as scents and sights, but she didn't want to take any chances. The small black cat hopped up onto Kassia's shoulders, nuzzling against her neck. They waited, watching as the horror approached.

The malefic crept closer, nose raised to the sky, sniffing the air—as though she were tracking them by their scent. The malefic paused just outside the witchshield, licking her lips as she squinted toward them. Kassia averted her eyes, afraid to make eye contact and somehow break through the barrier. Vines protruded from the witch's skin, looping around her limbs and sinking back beneath the flesh, pulsing with a dark and oily magic. She hissed, snapping her head one direction and the next. Then she was gone, crawling over branches and into the mountains.

And yet, Kassia was still afraid to breathe.

Rays of sunlight finally ended the long night, and they hadn't seen any sign of the malefic for hours. The three witches stood at the edge of the witchshield, alternating between staring at the protective barrier and searching the woods. It was time to move on, but as soon as the shield was down, they were vulnerable again.

Wrenn knelt to pick up her fluffy orange cat, crooning in her ear as she scratched her behind the head. "What do you think, Ylvanis? Is it safe?"

The cat purred before jumping down and stepping through the witchshield. She sat, licking her paw and cleaning her head. Finally, Ylvanis stood, flicking her tail.

"She says it's safe," Wrenn relayed.

"Did you name her?" Kassia asked, remembering how she'd been told it was rude to give a cat a name.

Wrenn laughed, a crystalline and musical sound. "No, she told me her name."

With a toss of her dark, curly hair, Wrenn clutched her crystal and stepped through the witchshield to join the cat. Kassia's brows pulled together, and she wondered what Wrenn meant by the cat had told her. Delphia shrugged and followed Wrenn. Exhaling, Kassia broke the circle with her toe and stepped into the grassy grove. Birds chirped. The sun danced off the snow-capped mountains. A small rabbit hopped through the grass. And when she felt down into the roots of the world, the energies were steady and unbroken.

It seems the danger has passed, for now.

The little black cat trotted over the toes of her boots before disappearing into the grass.

"Do you feel anything?" Kassia asked. "Any energy or magic? Any pull?"

Wrenn reached for her crystal and closed her eyes for a few minutes before she opened them again. "No, not yet."

"Should we keep going?" Delphia asked.

"I am going to try scrying for the place to plant the seed," Wrenn said. "Hopefully the crystals will guide us."

Wrenn knelt, drawing a circle in a small patch of dirt, and set a pebble, a few drops of water, and a leaf to signify landmarks. Quietly as ever, Wrenn unlooped the crystal pendant from around her neck, dangling it from her fingers. Ever so slowly, she began to drift her hand in lazy circles. Kassia leaned forward, watching for any sign of change. She couldn't sense any magic, but that was the untamed nature of wildecraft. Everyone accessed it entirely differently.

The crystal snapped to the north, straining against the leather strap. Wrenn allowed it to guide her hand across her makeshift map, until it stopped moving at a small depression in the dirt.

"Ah, I should have known," Wrenn murmured.

Kassia's pulse spiked with excitement. "Do you know where that is?"

"It's a crystal cave with a large skylight a few miles into the Warden's Watch Mountains. The crystals could work as a permanent protection shield!" Wrenn's voice, even excited, hardly raised above a normal speaking level.

Kassia almost smiled as a glimmer of hope cut through the grief and hopelessness.

The miles flew by, through the trees and rocks until they reached the base of the mountains. Wrenn followed a game trail into a narrow valley that was hardly the width of a wagon, hidden by two entwined oak trees—which looked strangely like a door. At the end of the winding valley, Wrenn wedged herself behind a large boulder in a slit that Kassia hadn't even noticed.

It's a perfect hiding place.

The rocks scraped Kassia's shoulder and hip as she slipped into the crack. Raising her hands as she stepped inside, she waited for her eyes to adjust to the darkness. Wrenn's hand found hers, guiding her toward the back of the cave. Kassia reached back to catch Delphia's hand—completing the circle of energy once more. They followed Wrenn through the winding passages that offered just enough light to avoid bashing their skulls into the walls. The dim light reflected off crystals inside the cave that were taller than a horse and wider around than a tree. Their sharp points angled every direction in a maze of translucent spears.

A bright ray of sun shone down from the skylight high in the cave's ceiling, so harsh that Kassia blinked against the sudden brightness.

Wrenn's voice was distant, though she remained right next to them. "This is the place."

Wrenn knelt before either of them could answer, quickly digging a small hole right in the center of the sunlight. She slipped the seed into the soil and covered it. Leaning forward on her knees, she began to chant.

Kassia was riveted to the sight, watching the seed find its new home and the witch who would tend to it. A wave of emotion crashed into her, and a tear slipped down her face. So many witches had sacrificed their lives to save them all. Salvation would rest upon the quiet acts of unknown women.

It was an honor to be part of this.

Delphia and Kassia clasped hands and joined in the prayers as they waited for the seed to sprout. Morning came again before a tiny green leaf pushed up through the dirt. Quietly, Kassia and Delphia backed away, leaving Wrenn to tend to her seed.

Kassia cast a single look back through the crystal cave before she set off. Already she felt the grief of losing the friend she'd barely gotten to know.

Heartspring

Chapter Nine

The bones of the forest remember.

— *Grimoire of the Wildegrove witch, Isenara, 673 N.T.C.*

Delphia and Kassia picked their steps carefully down the side of a steep slope as they edged closer to the Heartspring village. Kassia had once climbed to the top of this peak, and she didn't relish returning to it. Just miles to the west, the aftermath of battle surrounded the Flame Pillar. They'd never been able to remove all the bodies or broken war machines, so they slowly returned to the soil. The carnage was forever branded into her mind.

"We're here, but I still don't feel anything. Am I supposed to?" Delphia chattered on, pushing her fire-red hair out of her face as she stepped around a sharp rock. "I don't use crystals, and I don't sense any magic gathering around us. I'm not really sure what I am supposed to be feeling for."

Delphia had hardly stopped talking the entire week's walk to Heartspring, and Kassia had already gotten used to her constant musings. In fact, despite the fact that Kassia always craved the solitude of her little cabin, she was finding that she had grown to crave Delphia's company, and already Gwinifer and Wrenn's absence was a painful hole in her chest. On top of losing her grandmother, it was almost too much to bear.

"Is there any special place here? Somewhere rituals are done? A sacred space or convergence of great power?" Kassia asked.

Delphia bit her lip and twined her red hair around her finger. "I do most of my magic inside my home, but it's not particularly special."

Kassia thought about it for a moment. "Gwinifer was in tune with nature and planted hers in the middle of the forest beside a stream. Wrenn used crystal magic and hers was planted in a cave. What magic is strongest for you?"

Delphia fiddled with her pendant, and it hit Kassia immediately. "Your pendant, it's a bone? Where are your ancestors buried?"

"I can't believe I didn't think of it. We have a sacred cemetery. We don't do any magic there, but we're all laid to rest there." Delphia's eyes welled with tears. "Except my aunt. She won't get the chance to join us now."

An unexpected wave of grief gripped Kassia by the throat, and for several seconds, she couldn't breathe. Her chest worked, but no air filled her lungs as dread washed over her. Finally, it relented, and she blinked back the stinging in her eyes.

"Your aunt, my grandmother, and all the others will be together and linked to us forever," Kassia comforted. "I don't think even death can steal this link. Can't you feel her?"

Delphia closed her eyes, clutching the small bone around her neck. When she opened them again, she nodded.

"Let's go to the cemetery?" Kassia said as the winds picked up.

"*Wolves haunt the woods*," the wind whispered.

"We need to hurry," Kassia declared, urgency threading her tone.

Delphia dropped her pendant and lifted her linen skirts to hurry down the slope. They reached the bottom and entered the woods when a faraway howl echoed through the mountains.

"Hag's teeth," Kassia swore.

"It's just beyond those trees!" Delphia called.

Kassia stumbled on the hem of her skirt, and flower petals went flying in all directions as she fought to maintain her balance. She chased after the flash of red hair that darted down the path.

Another howl cut the skies, and Kassia glanced around for her cat companion. It had just been with her a moment ago. Angry spears of panic bloomed in her chest as she sent a quick prayer to the forest gods that the animal would be safe with predators lurking about.

A tall white wall came into view, and Kassia realized that it was made of sun-bleached bones. She didn't have time to ask whose bones they were or why there were so many before snapping and cracking branches nearby caught her attention.

Delphia reached the bone gate first and began chanting and rubbing ash across it in a series of patterns that Kassia recognized as ancient wards.

"Hurry!" Kassia urged her.

"I have to complete the spell to open it!" Delphia continued chanting and drawing runes as the sounds grew closer and closer.

Dread washed over Kassia, and she knew they were already too late.

A Mooncursed beast launched from the shadows and bit down on Delphia's ankle. Several heads taller than a man, it had a deformed wolf head with an elongated human body and metal plates affixed between tufts of fur. Its fangs sank deeply into the witch's flesh, and she screamed in surprise and pain. Kassia flashed back to the Mooncursed attack she'd barely survived, when it had been her ankle in the beast's mouth and someone had risked their life to save her.

Furious determination replaced her blood as she sprinted toward the beast. Delphia wouldn't die today. She wouldn't allow anyone else to be taken from her. Kassia's feet nearly flew across the ground as she reached into her satchel to grasp a handful of vials. She didn't even look to see which she'd taken as she came face-to-face with a monster that ought not exist. It released Delphia and opened its maw to roar at her.

With a flick of her wrist, she released the vials, and they broke across the beast's exposed, plated skull. It roared again in agony and stumbled back as flames erupted across its neck and chest.

Rising, Delphia's limbs crackled with the fury of unspent magic.

The hairs on Kassia's arms rose as Delphia brought herself to standing. Kassia could only watch as the other witch's temper unleashed on their wounded attacker.

Delphia's red hair floated upward, whipping around her like angry serpents. The inhuman, guttural scream that tore out of her throat echoed against the bones and headstones. Magic swirled around her fingers as she gripped a sharpened femur in each hand. Even her eyes burned a bright red, as though fire ripped through her soul.

She screamed again before plunging the femurs into the beast's neck. Blood sprayed across Kassia, Delphia, and the bone wall surrounding the cemetery. The Mooncursed twitched and spasmed until it stopped moving.

Kassia leaned back against the wall, trying to catch her breath for a moment, before she remembered Delphia's injuries and hurried to her side. Delphia had propped herself against the bone wall and was lifting her skirts to look at her shredded ankle.

"What was that?" Delphia panted through the pain.

"A Mooncursed, from the stories. The emperor of Demorra has created his own, mixing them with ancient magics, actually the same that created the malefics. Now hold still."

Kassia felt along Delphia's ankle, searching for broken bones. Finding none, she sighed in relief. The gashes continued to bleed, but at least she wasn't going to leave her friend alone in the woods to fend for herself for months or longer with a broken ankle.

"We'll wrap this up, and it'll be fine, thank the goddess," Kassia said, digging into her bag.

Finding the waterskin of Moonwater, she cleansed the injury to prevent her friend from turning into one of those horrid beasts. Her deft hands then wrapped gauze with mynt leaf, aloe, and crushed dawnrose. She wrapped a few more layers before tying it off. Crimson bled through for a few moments but finally appeared to stop.

Delphia's brow was damp with sweat, but to her credit, the tough witch had remained conscious and didn't appear to be in shock.

"What was that?" Kassia asked.

"What?"

"The magic?"

"Oh," Delphia replied, "I'm not sure. I've never tapped into that much before. Do you think it's because I'm supposed to plant the seed here?"

"Maybe. Or the land is awakening with more and more magic."

Delphia tried to prop herself up to standing, but Kassia stopped her.

"Don't put any weight on the ankle until we're sure the bleeding has stopped," Kassia instructed.

"That's probably a good idea," Delphia said.

Kassia helped her stand, lifting as much of her weight as she could. Slowly, they hobbled toward the gate, and Delphia finally completed the spell to open it. Entering, Kassia found herself surrounded by about an acre of headstones in various shapes and sizes.

Delphia pointed to an empty area just inside. "That seems as good a place to plant it as any."

"Can anyone else get inside of here?" Kassia asked.

"Only blood relatives of a witch buried here who knows the spell." Delphia lowered herself to the ground. "I didn't learn it myself until last year. I don't actually know if anyone else knows it."

Kassia exhaled in annoyance. "Why do they keep so many secrets?"

"Maybe it's the only way to really protect the knowledge?" Delphia mused.

"Or ensure that it's lost forever!" Kassia pinched her nose before forcing her emotions to calm.

"Can nature magic ever be lost? It's all around us," Delphia said.

She scooped dirt out of a small hole and placed her heartseed inside. It glowed for a moment before she covered it with damp soil. Just as before, they meditated together for hours until the seed awakened and pushed through the surface. The sensation of the sprout connecting to the network was stronger this time, as if Kassia could almost trace the web across Teridar.

Dawn arrived, and Kassia slid her pack over to Delphia. "We packed enough food for about a month, but you may need more with that ankle. Take my provisions." Delphia raised her hands to protest, but Kassia continued. “I can forage along the way, but you can’t.”

Delphia pursed her lips. “Thank you.”

Kassia slipped her satchel with only a few remaining vials over her shoulder. “Be safe. Send a raven if you need anything.”

“Good luck,” Delphia called.

Kassia pushed open the bone gate and stepped out into the quiet mountainous forest, hoping she didn’t meet any enemies on her return trip to Wildegrove.

Her heart ached as she left her final companion, feeling more alone than ever.

Ways of the Witches

Chapter Ten

Every witch should have a coven.

— *The Book of Covens.*

Grasping her protection charm, Kassia stood before the Way, a slim stone doorway thirty paces tall with iridescent, rainbow orbs of light floating within, as if you could step right into the stars themselves. But she knew the door would remain locked unless opened by magic. She could have pounded on the translucent veil for years and it wouldn't have made a difference.

"Please, Adonis," she whispered.

She'd managed to make it back by the date she'd promised, just barely. Having arrived only yesterday, she'd spent the night inside a witchshield, hardly daring to sleep. Yet, she didn't know if the sorcerer had received her message or could come. They'd fought Mooncursed side by side, traveled the length of the continent, grieved their slain friends together. But he'd never been the same after those attacks, and he was no longer an apprentice these days.

What if he doesn't come? I'll have to travel the entire continent by myself, and I don't have a horse. The trip would take months.

The small black cat with a white star wove between her legs, purring and arching its back as it nuzzled against her. She knelt to pet it.

"Why, hello. Did you walk all this way on your own?" she asked.

The cat didn't respond of course, but she never stopped speaking with it out of habit.

Out here, alone, she felt exposed, as though a malefic could attack at any moment. She shuddered. Their corrupted magic was an affront to everything she held sacred. And if she was right that they'd been tainted by the dark goddess, Niamh, then there was no limit to what they were capable of.

The Way shimmered, and Adonis stepped through, the portal transforming into a clear path to the other side through a curtain of light and magic. He wore the robes of a fully accepted sorcerer, and his brown, wavy hair hung across his brow, reminding her so much of his sister, Aurienne. He was taller and broader than he'd been when she'd last seen him several months ago. The Way closed behind him like a veil knitting itself together thread by thread.

Kassia smiled at the young sorcerer, relief pouring through her. "You received my message. Thank you for coming."

"Your raven was insistent." For the smallest fraction of a second, his eyes danced with warmth she thought he'd lost for good since the war had begun. "I am fairly sure it threatened to relieve itself on my books if I didn't read the note immediately. And it waited until I'd traveled to the Way before it left. I half expected it to come through with me to ensure I'd arrived."

Kassia allowed a small smile on her lips despite the numbness in her soul. "I nearly sent it with a bribe but wasn't sure what you would have accepted."

"Your raven was stubborn, but a sturdy book is about all I would want these days," he replied.

Gone was the carefree drunken youth, and in his place, a man still too young to have so much regret and determination. Her heart ached for him. He must still blame himself for the death of his mentor, and yet she knew she could offer no comfort. Her words would fall on deaf ears.

"I didn't want to put too much information in my letter in case it was intercepted." Kassia clasped her hands. "Would you be able to take me through another Way?"

He nodded. "Where do you want to go?"

"I have a special seed entrusted to me to plant in the Seven Forests to help protect us from Niamh's magic." She held up her rough map. "It's the only part of the continent that has no witches of its own."

"Of course." Adonis retrieved a map from his leather satchel, leaning in to study it. "There is a Way just south of the Bloodrose Spires. About two days walk from the heart of the camp there. It's the closest I can bring you."

"Perfect." Relief coursed through her. "You've saved me weeks of travel."

He returned the map to the bag. "I'll return in a week to bring you back."

"Thank you."

Adonis turned toward the Way, moving his hands in a series of gestures that timed perfectly with the ancient words he whispered. It shimmered again, opening to a woody grove on the other side.

Palm up, Adonis offered her his hand, which she accepted.

"Remember what happened to Aurienne inside the Way. We don't know what could be lurking within. The path is short but fraught with danger," Adonis warned. "And don't linger or you could be trapped."

Kassia's throat bobbed. It was not so long ago that Mathis had spoken the same words to their caravan, and yet it was a lifetime gone. Now he, too, was gone. How many would this war rip from them? She glanced at the stoic sorcerer at her side. And what would become of those that were left behind?

Forest Roads

Chapter Eleven

The forest always takes you where you need to go if you listen.

— *Forest wisdom.*

Oak, maple, and ash trees formed a wall at the edge of the Seven Forests, lined with wood ferns, mugwort, and stinging nettles. Kassia clutched her satchel as she trudged across the rolling hills, distinctly aware of how alone she was now that her witch companions had remained with their seeds. The long switchgrass pricked her arms as she navigated toward the tree line.

Since leaving Adonis and the Way, she'd walked about ten hours before reaching the wide river and the edge of the forests she sought. Her boots were heavy and sticky, and her dress and braid stuck to her skin. The sprawling forest city she'd visited when she'd accompanied Avyllon's caravan across Teridar was at the heart of the Seven Forests, leaving her at least another day of travel.

Water splashed her boots as she knelt to refill her flask in the shallow, fast rapids of the river. The icy liquid soothed the burning of her dry throat, and she splashed a handful on the back of her neck to help cool down from the summer heat.

Pausing, she sensed another link of energy snap into place. Another of the thirteen seeds had been planted. Hers was the final seed that remained unplanted. They were so close. And then that only left the key seed.

"*The one with a heart of the forest comes*," the wind whispered.

A warrior with brown skin, slightly darker than hers and covered in ink tattoos, stepped out of the trees. Over six feet tall, he wore animal leathers, and feathers were wound into his long black hair. He lifted the spear in his hand in greeting.

Kassia stood, smiling. It was Thaen, one of the Free Peoples of the Seven Forests. They'd traveled together with the Avyllon caravan last autumn when Theo had been gathering his allies to face the looming war. The Free Peoples never left these woods, and Thaen had been all too eager to travel to the capital to represent them with his father, Elder Dharek. A fearsome warrior, his infectious energy and lighthearted manner would be the perfect ray of light in these dark days.

As he approached, he said, "Kassia? I sensed magic in these parts but didn't expect to see you. What are you doing all the way out here?"

Thaen offered his hand, and she accepted it, but he drew her into a swift bear hug, keeping his spear hand off to the side. He chuckled as she detangled herself from the warm welcome. Why was she blushing already?

"Hello, Thaen," she said. "Adonis portaled me through the Way south of the Bloodrose Spires. It was the quickest means to get here."

"Did you miss me that much?" he quipped.

Kassia playfully rolled her eyes. He was always like this, unserious and joking. Hardly anything could steal his enthusiasm.

"Of course," she humored him. "Though, it wasn't what brought me here."

His brows pulled together seriously. "Another attack?"

"Oh no, not exactly." She exhaled. "Well, sort of. It's a long story. The short of it is that I need to plant a magic seed in the heart of your forests somewhere to provide protection against dark witches and magic."

"I see." He scratched his jaw. "Of course, you're welcome to do whatever needs to be done to defeat our enemies. It sounds like we'll need to head back to the main city. Why don't you tell me the long version on the way?"

A few hours later, they were nearing the heart of the forest. Thaen had somehow cut hours off the journey as he navigated them through the trees. She'd shared the events of the last few weeks, the news of her grandmother, the malefic witches, and her quest. She'd told of her new friends that she'd been forced to leave nearly as soon as they'd found one another. He'd said little, asking questions. She was surprised how easily the painful words had come.

As they walked, Kassia noticed Thaen rubbing his arm as though it bothered him. The skin had morphed into a tree bark texture that climbed up to his elbow on both arms. The warrior glanced at her, noticing where her gaze had landed.

"It's healing, slowly but steadily," he said. "The more I abstain from the naturalist magic, the more it goes away. At the same time Avyllon took back the Flame Pillar, Demorra sent its forces to try and burn our forests. It required more magic than we should've used. But another couple of weeks and maybe my arm will be back to normal."

"Does it hurt?"

"It stopped bleeding, so the worst of it is over."

That means it hurts, and he just doesn't want to admit it.

She said, "You sacrificed much to protect us all."

"It's worth it." He shifted his spear to his other hand. "I didn't sacrifice as much as some did. Allesan is now the last of his kind. All his kin have taken to root permanently in order to protect the next generation of saplings. And many gave the ultimate sacrifice, like my father."

"I heard he died during the battle," she said, reaching out to squeeze his arm. "I'm sorry."

Thaen lifted his chin. "He died valiantly protecting the ones he loved. We should all be so lucky to go out that way."

A deep sigh rumbled Kassia's chest, accompanied by sorrow. "My grandmother died in much the same way as Allesan's family and your father. She became one with the forest in order to give us a chance at protection. It seems nature is demanding sacrifices to fight this. Superstitions and old stories are coming to life."

"I'm sorry about your grandmother," he said. "She sounds like a formidable woman. I am sad that I never got to meet her."

Kassia allowed a small chuckle to escape. "She was formidable. You should have seen her fighting that malefic. You'd never have known how old she was. And so brave. She hadn't even seen monsters before, yet didn't hesitate." Her tone grew somber. "And she didn't once seem afraid or nervous when we went to the rite, even though she knew what she faced. She never hesitated to do what needed to be done. I have big shoes to fill."

"I worry about the same," he said. "My father was so respected and level-headed. Sometimes I wonder whether what I'm doing is right. It's so hard to lose your compass."

"Yes!" she exclaimed. "That's exactly it. I miss her terribly, but even worse, sometimes I don't know who I am without her. She made me who I am."

Thaen nodded, shifting his spear from one hand to the other as he stretched his shoulders. "I keep reminding myself that I honor him by continuing. And one day we'll meet and I can tell him everything I tried to do."

The ache in her chest lessened just a bit. "Oh, the stories we'll share when we meet them again."

"I only pray to the forest gods that I help as many as I can to live long lives. It's nearly impossible with all that surrounds the war."

"Everything changes every day," she agreed.

"Old magic awakens, as if fighting to cleanse itself," he said.

"And I feel as though we understand none of it," she continued. "This war just seems so big. We have kings and emperors, gods and goddesses, immortal elves and vampires and other beings that haven't been seen in thousands of years. Queens that rise from the dead. Our futures play out in the minds of seers who twist fate to their whim. I can hardly even comprehend it most of the time. I answered a call to aid in the aftermath of the Flame Pillar battle, and seeing the carnage, I can't imagine actually fighting in it, much less leading the charge. I survived a Mooncursed attack last year, and it was a fraction of the scale."

She stepped over a downed branch on the path, pausing to accept Thaen's hand as he helped her over.

"Yet, this war will be our end if we let it," she said. "It's too big for any one person to triumph. We all have a part to play, and I must give the defenseless townsfolk a chance."

"I agree. It's why my father and I pushed for us to join the alliance. It's going to take all of us."

Thaen paused, touching her arm to pull her back. "Let me help you. A Pillar fell once, and the emperor will be set on bringing them all down. If this protection spell could help keep people safe when he throws all he has at us, then we need it. Just tell me what to do."

Kassia looked up into his deep brown eyes, recognizing his dedication. "I need to find a safe place to plant a heartseed, and then I need to find where to plant the final heartseed key."

"We'll have to convince the elders if you want to plant such a thing within our borders." His jaw ticked even as his eyes danced with mischief that reminded her of her grandmother.

"Do you think they'll agree?" she asked.

"I guess we'll find out."

Seven Forests

Chapter Twelve

And then seven forests become one.

— *Unknown.*

The treetop city at the heart of the Seven Forests was every bit as beautiful as Kassia remembered, even with the damage from the fires that marred the eastern edge. As the curtain of living trees opened to allow them entrance, Kassia couldn't help but gawk at the hanging bridges connecting the treehouses.

"Assemble the elders," Thaen stated to several warriors standing at the gates. "The time has come."

With hints of smirks and knowing looks, the young warriors dispersed through the city.

"What is the meaning of this?" an older looking man demanded as he stepped into the sunken meeting area.

Other older men and women, who must be their elders, Kassia realized, encircled Thaen as a growing crowd leaned out of treehouse windows and tree-bound stairways and surrounded them.

"They're always grumpy." Thaen winked at her before taking the center of the meeting place. "There is news to share and consider," he said to the elders. "Kassia is a witch from the Wildegrove and seeks to plant an enchanted heartseed within our borders to complete a continent-wide protection spell."

"We are naturalists. Wildecraft is not our way," a female elder with long, white hair replied.

The woman had no bark on her arms—indicating that she hadn't used her magics to help fend off the fires that Thaen had lost his father in. Her brows lifted as she realized that the politics and acrimony here might be deeply rooted. If the elders hadn't even been willing to sacrifice to save their homes . . . It suddenly occurred to her that there was more going on.

What is he planning?

An elder with a shaved head leaned forward with a sneer. "How do we know that this isn't a trick?"

Anger flared inside of Kassia. "Excuse me. *I* fought our enemies instead of hiding here hoping they wouldn't find me. And even when they did, I don't see that you fought back."

She instantly regretted her words and bit down hard enough that her cheeks hurt.

"Outsiders can't be trusted." The man looked directly at her when he spoke.

"Many homes were burned before we pushed back the attack," Thaen countered. "If this could provide protection to us, we need to do it. We will sense if the seed is malicious."

"No. The answer is no," a man with large feathers braided into his gray hair answered.

"I don't believe you speak for us." Thaen's jaw ticked, an expression Kassia hadn't seen on him before. "My father died protecting us, and his replacement hasn't been voted on yet."

"Take the seed somewhere else," the elder replied.

Panic raced through Kassia. If she couldn't plant her seed to complete the spell, the issue of the key seed aside, then all those sacrifices would have been for nothing. This was the only region without any seed—this had to be the last location.

Kassia grabbed Thaen's arm and whispered in his ear, "It really should be planted somewhere in the Seven Forests."

"Elders, will you permit the planting somewhere in our forests?" Thaen asked.

There was a particular finality about his words, as if he were offering one last chance. But she didn't understand it.

"No." Many elders spoke at once. "The seed shall not be planted here."

No. No. No.

Am I going to have to sneak in?

Is there a spell I can use to hide it?

Kassia's mind raced to overcome this denial, but she noticed Thaen hadn't reacted as she expected. She'd thought he might get angry or shout, but he did neither of those things.

Thaen merely nodded, as if anticipating their response, but he still seemed disappointed.

"I hadn't planned to do this yet, but it seems the time has come," he whispered to her.

What?

Bitter resolve crossed his face as he spoke. "I know I am not an elder and have no right to call for an assembly, but perhaps that is the issue," he said. "Our traditions are steeped in generations of familial bonds bringing us together, but what will they matter if we're all dead?"

The elders' faces grew red as Thaen spoke.

Thaen continued, "My father is dead. He died protecting us, and it was hardly enough. If Avyllon hadn't managed to relight the Flame Pillar, we would have burned. In these times of war, we need a chieftain—someone who can make quick decisions about the protection of our people. Perhaps if we'd had more decisive leadership during the attack, my father would be alive. All those we'd lost in the confusion and uncertainty might be here."

Many of the younger warriors whooped and hollered as he spoke, cheering at his words. Even some of the older people exchanged curious glances at the proposition.

"And that chieftain should be me," he said. "I proved myself in battle. My father trained me my entire life for this. I've been to Avyllon and seen our terrible foes. None is better prepared to lead us in what comes."

Kassia's mouth fell open.

Oh, my goddess. What is he doing!

She glanced between the elders and Thaen as her cheeks flushed with embarrassment, as though she were eavesdropping on a conversation not meant for her.

An old woman hissed at him, "You shouldn't even be allowed to speak. Chieftain? You must be mad."

Thaen lifted his hands. "This is a matter for all of us. It's our children, our home, our lives. I call for a vote of *all* our people. Do you want a chieftain to lead us in matters of war? Raise your hand."

Hands shot up into the air. Obviously more than half, perhaps more than three-fourths of all those gathered—even a few elders. Kassia lifted a brow. This had been too easy. Thaen must have been working on this for a long, long time.

Half the elders whipped their heads around in shock, various levels of anger and indignation on their faces. They hadn't expected his plans or the support he would have. And he'd called for the vote so quickly that they hadn't been able to stop it.

What a mastermind. He will make a fine chieftain.

"You fought valiantly in the attack, and it seems you have the support of your people." An elder picked his words carefully, eyes darting around him. "As Dharek's son, you were always meant to take his title and were trained accordingly. In your father's memory, I trust that you can lead when it comes to matters of war, but remember that in matters of the clan, the elders maintain authority."

Thaen's smirk was thin, but he said, "I plan to do my father proud. My first decision is planting a heartseed from the Wildegrove in the center of our settlement to complete the wildecraft protection net around Teridar." He glanced in Kassia's direction. "We must support our allies. We're stronger together."

Kassia waited until the elders and crowd dispersed and they were alone once more to ask, "How long have you been planning this?"

"Since before my father passed. The elders are hanging onto a way of life that no longer exists. They're still living in a world that has changed and left them behind. If we want to survive, we have to move forward, and that means taking some risks."

Apprehension tickled Kassia's neck up into her cheeks as she followed the tall warrior to the large sunken meeting area in the center of the settlement. "I didn't mean to bring trouble here."

He shrugged, too at ease with what he was about to do. "The elders would know if your seed was planted. I can sense its power from here and it lies dormant. You must have their permission. You brought no trouble here; you have only brought power to fight the darkness, and they must be willing to accept it."

"Don't do anything rash on my account," she said.

The slow grin that spread across his mouth was different, and his eyes lingered a moment too long. "Perhaps you inspire reckless behavior."

Her cheeks heated. Thaen was flirty by nature, but this felt different. Had she simply not noticed before, or was this new? She tilted her head back to look up into his eyes as he took a step closer, before they both flushed and looked away.

Her heart fluttered for a fraction of a second with hope.

Dawnrose
Chapter Thirteen

Not even dawnrose can heal a broken heart.

— *The Healer's Book of Kassia Guara, witch of Wildegrove.*

Leaning over the balcony overlooking the settlement, Kassia lost herself to the steady thrum of the city. She adored her quiet cottage home, but she found the energy of this place invigorating.

Footsteps signaled an arrival, and she glanced up to see Thaen walking up the treehouse bridgeway. He handed her a steaming mug of tea and leaned his forearms on the living branch railing beside her, sipping his own mug.

"Good morning," he said. "Did you sleep well?"

She swallowed and took a taste to hide the blush creeping onto her cheeks. "I slept perfectly, and you?"

He didn't answer. Instead, he just smirked and drank his tea as they looked out over the bustle of activity below them. Even at this early hour, parents were teaching children crafts and trades, warriors sharpened their spears, and teachers were instructing group lessons on magic in the streets while others traded items with one another.

"For how busy it is, it's so peaceful here," she said.

Thaen straightened and surveyed the people below. "We were blessed for a very long time."

Kassia sipped the sweet, amber liquid. "I could see why you all had no reason to leave the forests for so long. Why the seclusion after your magics emerged wasn't so terrible."

"*The heart always knows a home*," the wind whispered.

Thaen cleared his throat, swirling his tea in his mug. "Can I ask you something? If it's too personal, please tell me. Are you and Saryll still . . ."

He trailed off when she shook her head, saving her from the rest of that painful sentence. But ire built inside of her anyway.

Kassia remembered it all too well. She had been in one of the greenhouses in Avyllon when Saryll had walked in, asking for lavendiir palm tea for Aurienne—even after everything. The seer had worn the ceremonial gown, stitched with constellations, moon phases, and the third eye of her goddess. She remembered her heart lurching as she waited for Saryll's response to her question.

"I'm going home. Will you come with me?" Kassia had asked.

Saryll's seer-clouded eyes had been impossible to read as always. "You know I can't just leave."

"You traveled the entire continent. How is this any different?" Kassia remembered the vexed words falling out of her mouth.

"I could travel with you for a time, but I will always be called back here, to the Triple Goddess. And she could send me anywhere." Saryll picked at her nails, expression tight. "I would never live elsewhere for any long period of time."

Kassia remembered the bolt of pain as she already knew that whatever they'd briefly shared was already over. "You could never live in Wildegrove, you mean?"

Saryll had tilted her head to catch Kassia's gaze. "As much as I'd like to, I swore oaths to my goddess. I bear her gift. I'm meant to be here. I can't live the rest of my life giving readings to the same few people in the same small town. She'd take my gift or worse."

Saryll had looked away, brows furrowing as her gaze had gone distant.

"Because your duty is greater than mine. You're more important," Kassia had snapped.

"It's not like that."

"I hear you," Kassia had said. "You need to give all your powerful readings to the city people, not to some small town in the middle of nowhere."

"My life is not my own," Saryll had said. "I hope you never understand what that is like."

Damn my stupid heart.

Returning to the present, Kassia glanced toward Thaen. "I should've known better than to chase that flirtation, but the magic in the wildecraft festivals is potent and brought us together for a short time. The seers' devotion to their goddess is too great, though, and Saryll was never going to leave that life." Kassia gripped her mug tighter. "And I wasn't going to try and be anything other than who I am."

Thaen angled his body toward her as he caught her gaze. "Well, she's a fool to have been blind to what was right in front of her."

All thought left Kassia as she realized that she hadn't been imagining his interest these past days. She stammered, unsure of what to say or how to respond. She'd been burned before, and he lived so far away. How was there a future in it?

He wasn't deterred by her silence. "I would never make you feel anything less than what you are."

Kassia nodded, feeling a blush darken her brown skin. She pushed a curled lock of black hair out of her face as she hid behind her mug.

"If you're ready, let's get this seed planted." Thaen placed his mug on a small table outside of the room she'd been staying in. "Are you coming?"

Quickly, she set hers down beside his and followed him through the maze of bridges and stairs, all the way down to the ground level.

"We're essentially in the center of the city. Where do you want to plant it?" he asked.

Kassia took the smaller heartseed out of the pouch around her neck, leaving the key seed, and covered it in her palms as she closed her eyes. She took a handful of steps to the north and then to the east before her eyes popped open. Somehow, she just *knew* where that last seed wanted to go. She understood what the other witches had said.

"Here," she directed.

This was a good place. Here in the heart of the city, it would be well guarded and provide the full strength of whatever protection it grew to all the inhabitants.

Kassia knelt and dug a hole a few hand lengths deep then placed the small seed within. It must have been her imagination, but she thought she saw it wiggle into the soft dirt as if settling into its new home. After it had been covered and soaked with Moonwater, she crossed her legs and sat on the ground. Kassia reached for the threads of energy zipping between the roots underneath them and guided them toward the small seed.

She began to meditate.

Thaen sat beside her silently, not even asking questions as he crossed his legs and rested his hands on his knees. Seven Forests folks passed by them, some stopping to watch for a few minutes before moving on, others paying them no heed at all.

Afternoon arrived before Thaen tapped her on the shoulder, breaking her from her concentration. "We should eat and rest."

Blinking, she tore herself from the energy threads below the earth and forced herself to release them.

"Maybe I can help another way?" he asked.

She knew immediately what he meant—his magic.

"I can't ask that," she said. "Your arm is just starting to heal. If you do, the transformation will begin again, and it'll be months before it's gone."

Thaen lifted his hands, and magic gathered around them. "We at least need to mark its location and keep curious children from digging it up after you're gone. And if I'm already doing a bit of magic, I might as well help it along."

Kassia hesitated. Many witches had given up their lives to create this protection, and the sooner it was working, the better. Especially if malefic witches lurked in the woods. Yet, she still hated asking Thaen to sacrifice so much.

Nearby clusters of sunrise-colored dawnrose quivered as Kassia prepared to agree.

"Don't you start," Kassia whispered to the plant.

Thaen glanced between her and it as if he could sense the interaction.

Our magic is so similar and yet so different.

"Are you sure you aren't a naturalist?" Thaen quipped, digging his hands into the pockets of his green, woven pants.

Kassia wiped her hands on her floral dress. "Just a healer with a touch of wildecraft."

"Nature doesn't respond like *that* to just anyone," he said. "You've got some of the power in your blood."

Even with her aching heart, his grin was contagious, and she replied, "Or the plants are excited to have wildecraft practitioners in their forest because we're less demanding than you naturalists."

"How do you want to mark this place?" Chuckling, he rolled his shoulders and placed his hands over a nearby dirt patch. "Pick a seed."

She tapped her chin. "Something challenging. Nightflame? I could use it for my brews."

Thaen grinned. "I could grow it, but then it'd be here waiting for someone to stumble on it."

"How about a ring of elder rose?" she asked.

"One of the pickiest flowers to get to bloom." He wiggled his fingers. "You know your stuff. Alright, let's do it."

Kassia placed a small, cracked seed into the dirt several paces from the heartseed's location and stepped back. Thaen's brow furrowed as he focused on it. Nothing happened for a moment. Then, the smallest green tendril broke through the ground. It rose, twisting and growing as thick as her wrist, but it didn't stop there. Roots burrowed into the soil, and another tendril emerged through the ground. A dozen more broke through, creating a solid ring.

Kassia's feet brought her closer of their own accord. Distantly, she could sense the prickling energy flowing from the land into Thaen and into the elder rose.

The vines twisted and braided themselves together into a growing ring, rising high above their heads. It burst into a wall of purple flowers with light pink starbursts staining the center. The soft petals rained down on them. Grinning, Thaen withdrew his hands.

"Amazing," Kassia breathed.

Kassia turned to smile at Thaen and noticed a small patch of bark growing from his upper arm that hadn't been there just minutes ago. He noticed her gaze and tugged his sleeve down. She caught his eye, but he only shrugged.

"It'll go away in a few days." He cracked his fingers. "Now, for your heartwood seed."

If the magic before had been a trickle, now it was a torrent. The heartwood seedling pushed through the ground and reached upward until a small sapling stood in the middle of the elder rose ring. Thaen stopped as sweat beaded down his brow. The bark was up to his shoulder on the other arm now.

"Thaen!" she exclaimed, putting her hands on his arm to examine the wound.

He ignored her concern. "What do we do with it?"

"You can make charms with the extra branches. A small pendant worn around the neck creates protection against some darker magics, once the net is complete."

"I can send my warriors to the other seed locations to raise at least saplings. Would that help?" he asked.

Kassia placed her hands into the dirt, tracing the energy lines that were now branching out in a maze, each seed connected to all others. This was the last one, save the key in the pouch around her neck. Yet, she knew that the magic wasn't active. Secretly, she'd been hoping that it would begin to do its work without figuring out what the key did, but no such luck.

Kassia bit her lip. "I have to plant the final seed—it's the key to it all. Yet, I have no idea where." Doubt crossed into her mind that she could really do this.

"Give me a map and I'll send naturalists out," he said. "Where are they located? Avyllon's and Rodarri's cities?"

Kassia shook her head. "They're mainly in small villages around the outskirts. I think we let the kings and queens worry about the big battles and the matters of state and politics, but we need to focus on the villages and people that can't protect themselves. But if you wouldn't mind, it would help to get the seeds growing."

She produced the map from her dress, and he took a quick look at it, memorizing the locations.

"I'll help you plant the key," he said.

She just looked at him. "You can't come with me. You're the chieftain."

"A chieftain would never ask others to do what he wasn't willing to do. And if we need to grow that one, I'll do it and just deal with the consequences or not use my magic for a while to recover." He shrugged. "We'll figure that out when we come to it."

"Thank you," she said. "I mean it."

"I would do it for any ally, but I'm happy to do it for you," he replied.

The look he gave her was pointed, and she wanted to believe him, but she hesitated. She'd hoped for love once and it had evaporated into morning dew before her eyes. When destiny called, few could ignore the demands. Yet, she so badly wanted to believe him.

"How long can you stay?" he asked.

"Adonis returns for me in a few days," she informed him. "I better leave the day after tomorrow, in the morning."

She wrung her hands, allowing her thoughts to wander.

He brushed the dirt off his palms as he said, "I'll be ready to leave with you."

"Are you sure?" she asked.

"Yes." His eyes promised that he meant it.

She smiled.

Maybe I'm not as alone as I thought.

Wicked

Chapter Fourteen

Wicked dreams and wildecraft words,
False promises and malefic curse.

— *Children's skipping rope song.*

Another Way shimmered to life, and Kassia, Thaen, and Adonis stepped through. Rolling hills led to snow-capped mountains, and the scent of northern pine trees filled her nostrils. Yet, the last seed in the pouch at her neck, the one her grandmother had told her would be the key, remained dormant.

"Brookhaven is the last Way in Teridar." Adonis adjusted his robes. "If you're not meant to plant the heartseed here, there's nowhere else I can take you."

Kassia pulled out her rough map of the continent, studying the purple smudges where she'd marked the heartseeds. "There aren't any glaring holes in the pattern."

"Maybe it's not like the Pillars where it's geographical protection. Maybe it's something else?" Adonis asked. "Where would witches hide something important? Is there anywhere with magical significance in wildecraft?"

The Tangled Root Grove was the only place that came to mind. Why would they give her the seed and not tell her to plant it there or plant it themselves? It wouldn't make sense to send her on this wild, futile chase around the continent when the stakes were this high.

It has to be somewhere else.

"I'm sorry for dragging you all over," she said to the sorcerer. "I really thought I would *know* where it was supposed to be, but I have no clue."

She pursed her lips as grief slipped into her chest. Her grandmother would know exactly what to do. Lorayne wouldn't have fumbled in the dark, searching for clues.

"I guess we go back to Wildegrove," she said. "I'll regroup and see if I can discover what I am supposed to do with the final seed."

"I'll go with you," Thaen offered. "I would love to visit Wildegrove afterwards as well. You've seen my home, and now I want to see yours."

With a few slashes of his hands, Adonis opened the portal.

Standing outside the glimmering Way, Kassia waved to Adonis. "Thank you! I owe you."

Adonis nodded, seriousness alight in every feature. "Good luck."

The Way closed.

Kassia turned to Thaen, who was smiling at her.

"Lead the way," he said.

Nearly back at the cottage, Kassia and Thaen strolled through the woods, taking the overgrown path from the forgotten Way back to Wildegrove. A crushing sense of foreboding settled on her as fog rolled through the undergrowth. She looked around, really looked, at their surroundings. A gleam of white caught her attention from a nearby oak tree. Drawing nearer off the path, she approached it. She couldn't quite make out what it was until she brushed off the layer of moss. A human skull was embedded into the very trunk.

Her eyes dropped to the forest floor, searching for other abnormalities, finding misshapen mushrooms, trees growing out of other trees, and strange, black, bulbous growths. And the rotten scent of honeysuckles hit her.

Backing away, she whispered, "Don't touch anything. We need to get back, now."

Kassia returned to the road and assumed a brisk walk. She slid her hand into her satchel and rifled around for the vials within. Thaen lengthened his strides to keep up, spear in hand, head swiveling around as he must have sensed her restlessness.

"*The woods are not safe tonight*," the wind whispered in her ear.

Lifting her skirts, Kassia picked up the pace. There was something very wrong here. Cackling echoed through the trees, and Kassia cast fearful glances over her shoulder.

"What's going on?" Thaen asked.

"I don't know. Something is wrong . . ." She trailed off.

A coven of nine hooded malefic witches emerged from the cover of the trees, grinning wickedly with smiles as sharp as knives.

Coven

Chapter Fifteen

Don't let the malefic witches catch you, or they'll drag you into the woods and feast on your bones.

— *The Tale of the Malefic.*

The coven of malefic witches crept a step closer, hands splayed in preparation of their magic.

We can't fight a coven. One was nearly too much.

This wasn't a fight they could win, and they needed to warn the villagers so they wouldn't be caught unawares.

"Run," she whispered to Thaen before bolting down the road.

Crooked branches tore at Kassia's clothes and braid as she sprinted through the woods.

Thaen matched her pace for pace, brandishing his spear as he ran. "Who are they?"

"Those are the malefic witches." She panted. "We can't let them catch us."

She picked up her pace, darting between trees, over rocks, and through streams. Her wet skirts grew heavy as her legs burned, but she pumped them as fast as she could.

Howls and cackling continued to echo through the trees just behind them, and their presence raked at her back. Branches cracked to the left, and she veered away toward the right.

"Oh, little Wildegrove witch, all alone. Where have you been?" a witch called in a singsong.

"We've been waiting for you!" another called with a scratchy, thick voice. "We wanted to make sure you were here to see your village burn."

"You didn't think you'd get away with murdering our sister, did you?"

Sweat poured down Kassia's neck, and the vials slipped around inside her satchel.

"*Duck*," the wind whispered.

Kassia didn't hesitate. She grabbed Thaen's arm and dragged him to the ground beside her, slamming into the hardpacked dirt at full speed. A whistling dagger flew overhead, burying itself into a tree. Kassia darted to the left this time, pulling Thaen's massive frame along with her.

In the distance, the soft glow of lights from the village dotted the spaces between the trees. Candles in the windows, fires crackling in the hearths. If they could just last a few more minutes, they'd make it. But then, the flames erupted into a fiery inferno—far too immense for even a bonfire.

Distant cackles filled the night air, along with the screams from the villagers.

"No!" A strangled cry burst from Kassia's throat.

Skidding to a stop at the main town road, she looked on in horror as the village burned. People were stumbling out of their homes into the dark, holding one another and coughing up black smoke.

Kassia briefly gripped the vials in her satchel before releasing them. It was no use. She didn't have enough to kill all the malefic witches, but she could try to help her people.

She darted to the door of a burning house, slamming her shoulder against it before bouncing off. Thaen slammed the butt of his spear against the wood, and it swung inward in a shower of splinters.

Darting inside, she grabbed an older woman by the arm and started aiding her outside. Thaen ushered a man holding two small children out the entry before carrying a woman outside to safety.

Without stopping, Kassia ran to the next home and the next, trying to help people escape as cackling malefic witches on flying brooms dropped glass bottles of fire onto the unsuspecting village.

"Witches fly through cursed skies with the blood of the goddess, Niamh!" a witch screeched overhead.

Kassia froze, watching a malefic witch drag a man into the shadows, from which he didn't return. Helping people escape the burning homes wasn't enough. But she'd never seen the malefics' magic before and had no idea how to face it. Everywhere around her, flames were climbing toward the cloudy skies. Nothing was safe. People were running, crying, screaming. All of them needing aid.

Where can we go?

Where will they be safe?

Kassia's head whipped back and forth before she noticed the road leading to her cottage just around the bend. Home had always been where she'd felt safest, but with her grandmother gone . . .

Grandmother! We put the elements for witchshields around the cottage and the wildecraft festival field.

Kassia began to shout. "To the cottage! We can protect you! Hurry!"

She grabbed villagers as they passed, shaking them as she shouted for them to take everyone and flee to her cottage. Slowly, crowds began running that way.

Kassia sprinted through town, shouting and waving her arms. "Come with me!"

At the bend, she jumped up and down, screaming and pointing in that direction. Most everyone she saw was now coming to her, seeking guidance from the one who'd healed their maladies and tended to their needs.

She hesitated. She knew she needed to get the witchshield activated, but she didn't want to miss anyone.

"You go and do what you need to do," Thaen said. "I'll stay here until the last second and bring any stragglers I can."

She squeezed his arm. "Thank you."

Running, she joined the groups assembling around her cottage. She pulled several vials from her satchel and rested them on the ground. Then she began to dig frantically to reveal the witchshield channel that she and her grandmother had dug all those years ago.

The field beside her home was filling up with villagers, but she couldn't delay forever. Waiting, she watched as Thaen jogged down the road carrying two children.

Hurry!

Fear and guilt wracked her. She hoped they were the last of the people, but there was no way to be sure, and they were out of time. Any who were caught outside the witchshield would likely perish at the hands of the witches unless they were able to hide in the woods. She whispered a prayer for them.

A handful of malefic witches chased the group down the street, flying over the town so fast their bare feet hardly touched the ground. Across the field, several more witches stepped out of the trees, holding torches with purple flames. They were surrounded.

The villagers huddled in the field, clinging to one another as the monsters from their fairy tales encircled them, chanting and hissing as they boxed them in with no escape.

Kassia breathed out, summoning her focus and tapping into the energy of the roots below. All it took now was the right blessing and fire to summon the shield.

Please. Please. Please.

Whispering a prayer, she dumped the contents of a vial over the exposed shield line of crushed vetiver root, red salt, and white dust. With shaking hands, she struck a match, but it burned out at once. Her breaths came fast as she struck another, but it, too, failed to light. The third match ignited, and she quickly held it against the channel. Then she tossed a vial of inferno flower and nightflame within. The circle lit at once with orange and black flames before it burned out right after. Pressing her fingers to the white ashes, she chanted softly, whispering the ancient words of protection. The air popped as a haze rose around them all.

The witchshield erupted to life, creating a solid, nearly invisible wall around the cottage and adjacent field. A malefic witch approached slowly, licking her black lips as her eyes darted around the shield. Step by step, she lazily drew closer until her face nearly pressed against it. A fly buzzed out of her eye but was caught by a bullfrog that wiggled out of her hair. Twisted sticklike vines wove in and out of her flesh, and bones shifted beneath her dark skin.

Grinning until her mouth nearly split the skin at the corners, she dragged her charred talons down the side of the shield in a spine-chilling screech. She pushed back her hood, revealing her face.

Kassia froze—recognizing the woman.

“Oh, little witch, what have you done?” Kassia’s mother asked.

A Door Without a Key

Chapter Sixteen

Only a witch can open a locked door without a key.

— *Journal of Queensblood Rianne Charlotte Lenore of Rodarri.*

Horror slithered through Kassia as recognition fell upon her like an ax.

"Mother?" Kassia whispered, despite knowing she couldn't hear her through the witchshield.

"I know you're in there, my dear." Her mother dragged her dark claws across the invisible barrier, causing Kassia to gasp.

That rotten honeysuckle scent wafted toward her, and she realized that she hadn't been imaging it these past weeks. Her mother had been at the malefic attack, watching but refusing to take part. When she'd honored her grandmother's death, she had smelled it again. And again, when planting the heartseeds. Her mother hadn't wanted to hurt her. Perhaps there was hope?

"What happened to you?" Kassia whispered.

"I've finally returned for you. Won't you come out and greet your mother?"

Kassia's stomach roiled. She thought she might be sick.

"We'll wait," her mother whispered as she backed away.

Kassia could only stare at the ghost of the person she'd once loved more than anyone in the world.

The witching hour came as the malefics dragged their talons along the witchshield, testing it for weakness. They chanted hexes, curses, and spells of undoing, before hurling purple balls of dark energy. Pacing, the coven eyed the villagers and Kassia like delicious prey. Her mother circled, searching for mistakes in the shield she'd once helped to create. When Kassia could no longer watch, she returned inside.

Once there, Kassia scrawled a series of notes onto a handful of paper. She wrote to every ally she could think of, praying they would come. She released a whistling note, and then another and another in a song. She repeated it several times until a flock of ravens swooped in through her open window. Attaching the notes to their legs, she petted their shiny heads before sending them off. They meant those inside no harm, so they'd be able to slip right through the protections.

The small black cat with the star leapt up onto the counter, curling around her hand and nudging at her. She petted it out of habit, lost in thought, well, really just lost. Her mother's return shook her more than she'd thought possible.

"Do you think they'll reach anyone in time?" Thaen asked.

"No," Kassia answered truthfully. "It's a matter of hours, not days, before the malefic witches crack through the shield, and then it'll be too late. I have to send the pleas, but we can't wait for that to save us. We have to save ourselves."

"What do you want to do?"

"We have to figure out a different way to save the people or we're all going to die. My magic isn't strong enough to face them. Even with my most powerful brews, I would need ingredients I don't have."

"I could grow them for you?" he offered.

Her heart melted a little from knowing what he would be sacrificing. Yet without hesitation, he offered to endure lasting pain to help her.

"Thank you, but I don't even have the seeds." Kassia placed her hands on the counter. "And I still don't know what to do with the heartwood key. If I could get the protection web working, we wouldn't have need for anything else, but I can't figure it out." She took a steadying breath, as her voice had risen to a frustrated shout.

"Are there other spells you can use?" Thaen asked.

"None I know." Kassia's head snapped up. "But my grandmother's grimoire may have other secrets."

"Where is it?"

She slumped. "My grandmother never told me exactly, only that it was hidden somewhere in these woods behind a locked door and without a key."

"From what you've told me of your grandmother, she would have made sure it was protected," Thaen said. "Wouldn't it be inside the witchshield? Why create a protection barrier and then put your treasured knowledge outside it?"

Kassia blinked. "Thaen! You're a genius!"

He blushed and grinned, but her brain was now racing through memories.

"My grandmother would have made sure I knew where to find it, and you're right—it would be well protected." She ran her hand across her face. "A door without a key? The front door to the cottage locks, but it has a keyhole and key. The other doors don't have keys, but . . ."

She crossed the floor to inspect each of the bedroom doors, running her hands across the wood, searching for any seams or runes. Finding none, she backed toward the center of the cottage, spinning a slow circle.

"A door without a key. I have no idea. There aren't any other doors anywhere." Kassia's words faded.

There was one other door just outside in the garden. One she'd nearly forgotten about.

"A door that's not a door," she whispered.

"It sounds like what we're looking for." Thaen chuckled.

Collecting a torch, Kassia stepped out into her garden and followed the cobblestone paths to the pair of old trees that twisted together just above head height, forming a narrow arch that she could hardly squeeze her thin frame through. It might not look like much now, just two trees that had grown too closely together. But to a child, it had been a magical door to the fairy realms, and she remembered the fantasy stories she'd lived out as a girl. An old, dried-up flower crown hung from one of the lowest branches, bringing a smile to Kassia's face.

Leaning forward, she peered between the two trees, seeing only her garden on the other side.

If it's a door without a key, how do you open it?

Could the seed be the key? Kassia lifted the small pouch over her head and held it out between the two trees, but nothing happened. She sighed. It would have been too easy. She returned the heartseed key to her neck.

"The seed is only the key to the heartwood protection spell. It doesn't open the door to my grandmother's grimoire," she said with disappointment.

Thaen lifted his head in understanding. "What else would be the key? She wanted you to have this, so it would be something you have."

Just then, Kassia noticed small, white crushed stone dust in the space between the cobblestones.

Cloudstar quartz?

What was it doing here?

Then she remembered. Her grandmother had her use the cloudstar quartz to reflect the light onto the path to find the correct one.

Lorayne had said, "Once you've been there, you won't need to do this again."

Kassia took a steadying breath. Perhaps for her, now that she'd already used cloudstar quartz and had been to the Tangled Root Grove, maybe she could follow the secret paths through the forest, including this one.

Placing the flower crown on her head for luck, Kassia exhaled and stepped toward the door. She pushed herself between the two trees and bark scraped her back. Her head hardly fit as she wedged herself through.

And then she stumbled into a spiraling room with walls made of a single tree trunk.

It worked!

There was a small, secret place tucked between the two trees, and in the center of the room was a single book on a pedestal.

Tears sprung to her eyes as she approached her grandmother's grimoire. The scent of lilies wafted through the air, and it felt as though Lorayne were here in this room with her. Stroking the corners of the pages, she paused, savoring the sensation of being close to her grandmother.

Kassia tried to remove the book, but it wouldn't budge. She would have to read it here.

With a breath, she opened it and began flipping through the pages. Several spells caught her eye, and she took pains to memorize each one. It would give her a fighting chance against the malefics when the time came.

There was no time to read every spell or page, and Kassia promised herself that she would return and learn the rest. If they survived. Time was running out, and though she could have stayed in there forever, she had much to do.

Kassia had nearly finished her searching when she stopped at the title of the last spell in the book.

A spell to increase one's magic.

With a gasp, she sat straight up. It was perfect. If she could increase her magic, maybe she could grow the ingredients for the spells she needed. If she couldn't figure out how to use the key, then wildecraft was all she had to deter the malefic witches.

> Increasing your connection to nature will enhance your abilities and increase your pool of magic.

And then her eyes fell upon the next line of the spell.

How to bond with a familiar.

Kassia slowly looked to the little black cat with bright eyes and a white star on its chest that was sitting on the floor of the secret room, flicking its tail at her.

FAMILIAR

CHAPTER SEVENTEEN

The forest has eyes, and the wind keeps secrets.

— *HIGH SEER AURIENNE AZARRAH, PROPHETIC VISION.*

Berry-stained drawings on the grimoire pages seemed to come to life as Kassia glanced between the instructions and the small cat. It hadn't moved in minutes, and she wasn't sure the creature had even blinked.

A familiar can increase the power of a witch. Before a familiar can be bonded, the witch must ask its permission. This brew will allow the requestor to temporarily understand the potential familiar's answer.

Would this brew allow her to talk to animals? Was that insane? She glanced back at the spell: "Combine the dust of cloudstar quartz, the charred root of a bloodrose vine, harvested thymewrinkle leaves, and crushed catmint petals. Mix with Moonwater and consume with the animal you want to bond."

Tapping her finger on the book, she locked eyes with the cat, wondering if she had lost her mind or was about to unlock secrets of magic she hadn't known existed.

"Hellsdamn it," she said. "Let's try this."

Kassia walked past the cat and out of the narrow doorway. She pushed through and stumbled out into the garden.

"You disappeared! Did you find it?" Thaen asked.

"I didn't find what I was looking for, but maybe I found something else. There's a spell I need to try," she explained. "Could you make sure the villagers are prepared while I'm busy?"

Inside the cottage, she rifled through the labeled glass jars until she found three of the ingredients of the spell and a flask of Moonwater. She gathered a stone bowl and stacked the items on one another as she returned to the garden. Balancing in front of the door, she knelt to collect a pinch of the cloudstar quartz in the mortar of the cobblestones. Turning sideways, she reentered the door.

Kassia set the bowl beside the grimoire and ground the components into a fine dust. Taking an apprehensive breath, she poured in the Moonwater and began to chant the incantation. The water turned to starlight, glimmering with silver and white clouds.

"Here goes nothing," Kassia said, tipping the bowl back and pouring half the contents down her throat.

The liquid was refreshing, with a minty, floral twang at the end, and it left a static sensation on her tongue.

The cat leaned forward to lap at the glowing potion, licking several rogue drops from its lips.

"Hello?" Kassia asked.

"*Hello.*" The cat's voice echoed in her head.

Kassia took a step back, hands coming up to the protection charms at her throat as she swallowed a gasp. She had only half believed it might work.

"*It's about time.*" The cat spoke, but his mouth didn't move. "*I thought you'd never get the hint.*"

Somehow, even as the cat spoke in her mind, his mouth was full of teeth—overenunciating the letter "t."

"I'm sorry," Kassia stammered. "I didn't realize it was possible to speak with you, or bond with you."

The cat flicked its tail, and she could almost sense the creature pursing his lips at her.

Kassia took a deep breath and bent low. "Will you forgive my folly? I am so pleased to make your true acquaintance. What is your name?"

The cat hopped up onto the pedestal, gingerly stepping over the fragile pages on silent paws. Kassia stood, trying not to cringe at the crinkling of paper.

"*I am Alastor.*"

"I'm sorry. I don't understand. Are you a cat?"

He audibly scoffed, a blend of hisses and low growls. "*Familiars are not cats. I took this form because it suits me, for now. Since your powers began to manifest, I've been lingering, waiting to see if you were worthy of the bond. Or if I should move on.*"

Kassia's lips parted in surprise.

"*Nocthar, your grandmother's familiar, always maintained this was a noble bloodline to partner with. It piqued my interest, and I've been watching ever since.*"

"My grandmother had a familiar?" she asked.

"*Yes, and many others who spent their time here while they waited to make their own bonds,*" he said.

"Why did I never know this?"

Alastor licked his paw. "*There is much you don't know. I always told Nocthar that Lorayne was keeping too much from you. She wanted to spare you the burden and keep the darkness at bay as long as possible. She knew the temptation it held.*"

Kassia's eyes watered. "And now I am woefully unprepared for what we face."

"*You have everything you need to be successful, if you figure out where to look,*" Alastor replied. "*Many witches before you have faced the same challenges. You must learn to trust your instincts.*"

Lifting her chin, Kassia said, "I would be honored to make that bond, if you so choose. You've been a steadfast companion, and I would endeavor to learn all that I have neglected to discover."

Alastor stretched back and then forward onto his small paws. "*I have already decided to accept. I was merely waiting for you.*"

Kassia grinned, relief thick in her chest. She read further down the spell and nearly gagged. Her hands shot up to cover her mouth as she reread and reread the passage.

> *The witch and the familiar will make an exchange. An eye for an eye. Ask the question, trade an eye for an eye, and heal with catmint.*

She glanced to Alastor. "It says . . ."

"*Yes, I will take your eye, and you will take mine,*" he said. "*It bonds us. I will see what you see and vice versa.*"

"How do we do that?"

Now Alastor was grinning. "*You cut out your eye, and I'll do the same. Are you sure you want to do this?*"

Kassia blinked, wondering for a short moment if this could possibly be a hallucination. Or a trick? Could this be a product of the malefic witches?

No. I've known this cat for years. I trust him.

Inside, she *knew* that this was the right decision. If she put aside the doubts and questions, her bones were at peace. Her blood was calm. There were no warnings from the winds or the ravens. The cat was her only remaining companion, and the bond would grant her increased magic to face the malefics. There was no other option.

"I'm ready," she said.

Kassia retrieved the knife from her belt, locking gazes with the cat. Alastor extended his claws.

"This would be easier with a mirror," she said.

"*It's better to go as fast as possible.*"

Frosty fear coated her veins as she angled the point of the blade toward her eye. Her limbs were leaden as her survival instincts screamed. It was a battle of will versus instincts. Her gut and heart knew that she needed to do this, but she was having a hard time convincing her hand.

She said, "I accept the familiar bond with Alastor."

"*And I accept the bond with the witch, Kassia.*"

Before she could convince herself not to, she drove the blade behind her eye and twisted a sharp circle. Molten sharp pain exploded in her skull, nearly sending her crashing to the ground as her vision was cut in half. Dark blood poured down her face as the eyeball fell out into her hand. She knew that it wasn't her actions alone with the blade—it was the spell beginning its work.

Alastor slashed at his own eye, leaving a gaping hole in its place. It rolled across the pedestal.

Biting down on a scream, Kassia placed her eye beside his before carefully exchanging them, wrapping his in the remaining catmint she'd prepared, and pressing the onyx orb into her empty eye socket. She held her hand over it, waiting, praying for something to happen. Alastor knelt forward, rolling her brown eye into his head before mirroring her and putting his paw over it to hold it in place.

A pop of air. A burst of light. Golden threads tightening around them. Blood and sinew creaking. And then it was done. The pain was gone, and she could see. Her vision was different, and all around her, she could now see far more supernatural images than ever before. Threads of energy wove between the trees and the people outside, connecting them all together. Colors were brighter, and splotches of light indicated where spells, hexes, or protection charms worked.

"There's so much more to the world than I ever knew," she whispered.

"*Now we won't need a potion to share each other's thoughts or vision,*" he said. "*We are bonded for life.*"

"Can I pet you still?"

"*That is agreeable.*"

She squealed, lifting him up and squeezing him against her chest as she planted kisses all over the top of his head. She couldn't help it. Her heart overflowed, and this was the only way to release it.

"*I did not agree to this!*" His protests were weak, and though he pushed her away with his paws, his claws remained sheathed.

Kassia placed him back down on the pedestal, seeing now for the first time his mismatched black and brown eye.

"Are you ready to get to work?" Her eyes, one now several shades darker than the other, gleamed with renewed hope. "We have potions to brew before the witchshield falls."

Alastor bared his needlelike teeth. "*I thought you'd never ask.*"

Witches in the Woods

Chapter Eighteen

Beware the witches of the Wildegrove.

— *Unknown.*

Locks of Kassia's hair escaped her long braid as she pushed the cork into the last vial she had. Every last one in the cottage had been emptied and refilled with as many witch brews and potions as possible. The carefully prepared herbs, spices, and components were spread across the counter, while the preceding contents littered the floor. With Alastor's aid, her magic had coaxed seeds to life, producing just enough of the coveted ingredients to brew her potions.

Warmth wrapped around Kassia as she remembered countless hours sitting at this counter with her grandmother. Lorayne had taught her everything she knew, and she owed the woman everything. Then she remembered her mother and horror crept back into her veins. A thousand questions rattled in her brain, but there wasn't time for any of them. She couldn't fail today. The sacrifices of all those witches must matter. No matter what she had to face.

Alastor picked his way between the vials. "*There is nothing else we can do. I sense the shield weakening. We are out of time.*"

"Do you know what I am supposed to do with the heartseed key?" she asked. "All of this seems futile without it. If I can even escape the witches, there will be no coming home."

"*That is knowledge I never acquired*," Alastor replied. "*What did your grandmother tell you*?"

"She said, 'It is the key. You'll know where to plant it, just listen to your heart.' And the door to the grimoire didn't react to it. I can think of nowhere that I haven't traveled to that makes sense to plant it."

"*We will figure it out*," Alastor reassured her, slinking out the window and into the garden.

Thaen walked in, ducking underneath the doorframe to avoid hitting his head. "Are you finished in here?"

"Yes. Take these. They are the most potent. We'll hit the malefics near the cottage hard to draw the attention of the others away from the wildecraft ritual field. The rest we'll give to the townspeople to aid their escape. Once they're in the woods, we need to run and hide."

"Where do we go?" he asked.

"I have no idea." She looked up at him apologetically. "I'm sorry you're involved in this."

He took her ink-stained hands. "I'm not. If I die killing evil witches across the continent, I will have done my part to weaken the empire, and I will have done so at your side."

Tilting her chin upward with gentle fingers, he stared deeply into her eyes. It made her heart flutter with unspoken promises.

"Besides, we won't go down without a fight," he said. "Perhaps they'll retreat before we do."

Exiting the cottage, Kassia surveyed the witchshield with her new eye. The energy was fading, and she knew they were out of time. The witchshield burned with flames of invisible energy, consuming the offerings at the base, but the fuel was about to run out.

Kassia strode out to the center of the field, the long grasses catching on her woven skirts. The villagers warily gathered around her, ash still smeared on their faces, casting looks back toward the malefics pacing not so far away.

"The witchshield won't hold much longer," she said. "Once it falls,

I will try to draw their attention away from you and onto me. You need to run. Run and don't look back. Go to our closest ally, Rodarri. There are bloodwitches there, and Queen Rianne will protect you."

"Why not Wyndsel?" a man asked. "It's closer."

Kassia clenched her jaw. "There are no friends there."

"Bloodwitches?" a young woman asked fearfully. "Aren't they evil?"

It was a common preconception, and Kassia herself sometimes wondered whether bloodwitches used a corrupted form of the magic she so dearly loved. There was no time for that now.

Kassia lifted her chin, speaking over the heads of the gathered. "Magic is only what the user makes of it. Rodarri has been a steadfast ally and protected its people and Avyllon from the invasion. You can't stay here. The malefic witches will kill you. And the bloodwitches will be able to stand against the malefics."

The villagers exchanged worried glances, but Kassia began to weave through them, pressing vials into their empty hands.

"When it happens, use these to create a fog that will hide you and run. Do you understand?" Kassia said. "Take your places at the eastern side of the field. I'll draw them to the cottage."

Finally, they all begin to nod, accepting her gifts with whispered thanks and edging away toward the field. The malefics watched, unable to hear within the witchshield, and paced in predatory circles.

The townspeople were crouched and ready, light packs already strapped on and children in their arms. Kassia stormed out toward the path before her cottage, watching her enemies. Her mother dragged her claws once more across the flickering witchshield as several others continued to chant dark incantations. The witches hunched forward like cats about to attack, circling the edges of the woods as the sun descended beyond the horizon.

Thaen was at her side, his hands already outstretched, and Alastor was flicking his tail beside them.

"I'm sorry this is how we begin our partnership," she said to Alastor.

Alastor flexed his claws and bared his small, sharp teeth. "*I'm not. Let's kill some witches.*"

And she believed he would.

"Are you talking to the cat?" Thaen asked.

A hint of a chuckle escaped her throat before Alastor's vision in his eye showed her that the energy of the shield had finally started to fade. The light dimmed all around them as it flickered once, then twice. She braced.

"Get ready to run," Kassia called over her shoulder.

The glass of the potions and brews clinked as she lifted her hands and prepared for the battle. The energy of the shield fizzled as a light mist of rain engulfed them.

The shield fell.

The Key

Chapter Nineteen

Witches are the heart of the forest.

— *Inscription carved into a fallen tree trunk beside the Wildegrove witch cottage.*

Malefic witches charged forward, but Thaen and the townsfolk hurled over a hundred vials straight for them. Smoke poured out of several witch brews, obscuring the cottage and surrounding field, while others sent fire or acid toward their foes.

At the final second, before the fog fully enveloped them, Kassia hurled a vial of inferno flower and nightshade berries at the nearest malefic witch. The malicious poison burst into flames that clung to her skin and clothes. The explosion knocked her back and sprayed blood across the witches beside her. Spinning, Kassia threw the second vial at her mother, who'd been taunting her these past hours, but she didn't see it break. And then everyone was lost in the fog.

Malefic witches hissed and screamed, flying across the ground to attack Kassia.

"Run!" Kassia screamed, hoping the townspeople were already racing toward the forest.

She glanced around, searching for her mother, expecting her to appear at any moment.

She's a malefic. If I have the chance, I can't hesitate.

Thaen called upon his magic, sending vines spearing toward the witches, wrapping around their legs and holding them in place. Vial after vial exploded in the fog as Kassia tossed them toward the moving shadows of the malefic witches.

The smoke cleared to expose an empty field, and Kassia nearly tumbled to her knees in exhausted relief. They'd made it out. Hopefully, the small protection charms and vials in their pockets would keep them concealed until they could reach Rodarri. The eight remaining malefic witches were craning their necks, snapping their heads between her and the tree line. She just had to keep their attention on her instead of them.

Kassia glanced at Alastor. "Do you have any tricks left? I have one vial of bloodrose and inferno flower remaining."

"*Light the cork before you throw it*," he said. "*It'll hit them hard.*"

"This is my last brew. After this, I'm running out of ideas," Kassia said.

Alastor twitched his furry ears. "*Then we run and fight from the cover of the trees. They will protect us.*"

Her mother stepped out of the fog, vines spreading across her face and arms. Her once beautiful braid was ragged and hanging down her back, with small creatures nesting within. She waited.

Looking at Thaen beside her, Kassia whispered, "As soon as I move, run."

Kassia held the vial over a lantern candle crackling on the stone wall beside her and then threw it into the face of the nearest witch. Realizing what Kassia was doing, the witch darted forward, whispering a harsh incantation that sounded like the words were fighting one another.

The vial exploded in a cloud of noxious green flames, and the witch toppled to the ground, writhing and screaming. The malefic's words hit Kassia just as hard, sending her flying and rolling across the garden beds. Sticks raked her face and arms, and rocks left bruises on her legs and hip. The fall knocked the wind from her chest, and she lay on the ground for a few moments, panting breathlessly to try and get any air into her lungs. Finally, she choked down a painful breath.

The witches were upon her. Kassia screamed as she scrambled to her feet, but they all stood over her already, as if they'd portaled—though she knew it was impossible. Her mother stood above her, features icy as she watched Kassia's pain.

Ropes of thorny bloodrose vines wrapped around Kassia's wrists and ankles as she struggled to free herself. The witches whispered incantations in that horrible hissing, grating language she didn't understand. The vines tightened on her, cutting into her flesh and growing up her arms. Her mother's jaw ticked, but she joined her coven in chanting.

Tears streamed down Kassia's face. Her mother wasn't going to save her. Despite hesitating to attack before, she was well and truly gone now. Any hope she may have had was dashed against the reality of her predicament.

Through the dark cloaks, she caught a glimpse of Thaen shooting vines toward a witch who cut each down before it reached her with a curving athame dagger. Bark was climbing up his arms and had reached his neck. If Thaen used any more magic, it might consume him entirely.

"Thaen, run!" she screamed.

Her words caught in her constricting throat as the witches' curse began to take root. It sapped her strength, her connection to wildecraft. She could sense those currents of magic, but they were too far away, and she had no brews, charms, or potions left—so it didn't matter.

Backing away, her mother grasped the lantern on the stones with her twitching claws. With a malevolent grin, she swung the flame toward Kassia's cottage. The lantern exploded in a hailstorm of glass, and flames erupted inside.

No!

All her fond memories went up in the blaze. The vision of her grandmother teaching her a charm for the first time burned until it was gone. The sunny days wearing flower crowns and running with other village children through the forest became a scorched mess that fled from recollection. All she could remember was every time she'd been alone.

"There is nothing in that cottage worth remembering," her mother hissed. "It was false promises of magic that always fails when it matters. It couldn't bring your father back after he died. They said it was *forbidden*. I had to leave to find magic powerful enough to save our family. You understand, don't you?"

Kassia's heart sank. Her mother had sought stronger magics to bring back her father, refusing to accept that such a thing wasn't simply forbidden, it was *impossible*. Wildecraft didn't work that way.

"You left me to go chasing after ghosts," Kassia said. "How could you?"

I can't give up now.

Wrenching her arms against the vines dragging her toward her knees, Kassia fought and squirmed, even as the thorns ripped into her flesh like a sawblade. Her mother grabbed her by the chin as the other witches continued their incantations. Kassia's blood began to slow. Her head snapped back, and green vines of light poured out of her mouth and nose.

In horror, she realized they were drawing her magic out of her veins. Tears poured down her cheeks as she tried to fight, but it was no use. Alastor launched out of the bushes beside her and landed on her mother's neck, leaving deep gashes across her face. Dark green blood oozed out of the wounds. Her mother caught hold of him with her own claws and hurled him to the ground. Alastor landed back in the bushes, hard. His little body didn't move.

"*Alastor!*"

Her mother reached out with her jagged talons to clutch Kassia's throat again and began to squeeze. "We can stop all of this. You still have a choice. You can join us."

Join them?

She has to be insane.

Why would I do that?

A little voice in the very depths of her skull whispered, "To survive." She inhaled as she fought against the fog beginning to cloud her thoughts.

Is this what their incantation is doing?

Thaen was nowhere to be seen now. She knew he wouldn't have listened to her and run away, and she prayed he hadn't been taken down by the malefic he had been facing off against. Alastor still hadn't moved, and she couldn't reach out to stroke his fur and check on him. Her heart ached as the reality of her situation set in. She'd always known these were difficult odds, but somehow, she'd always believed that this wasn't the end.

The witch released Kassia's neck. "You'll never be alone again."

Kassia's breath hitched as her mother had found her weakness and pressed right into it. She'd been so lonely since her grandmother had passed, second-guessing everything she did, wishing that she had someone else to lean on. That small child who sat alone in the garden wondering when her mother would return came racing back. Maybe if she joined them, she could save her? Her mother's intentions had been true, so what if there was enough left of her to help?

The seeds.

The spells.

The key.

All of it was too much.

"You'll have a coven and sisters," the witch continued, whispering into her ear. "And we'll be with you always. We would never, ever leave you, not for a moment."

A sob wracked Kassia's chest as all the grief she'd been holding onto for her grandmother burst forth like a collapsing levee that threatened to wash her away.

"We have become one with nature in a way that you can't possibly imagine." The malefic witch was staring into her eyes now, as though hypnotizing her. "We're going to unlock all the secrets of magic."

The malefic witches aren't doing anything wrong.

They are just trying to learn more powerful magic.

The attack was only to avenge their sister, a misunderstanding.

The thoughts clouded Kassia's mind, as somewhere far away her body screamed in pain. The power continued to waft out of her mouth, nose, and one eye, and now her ears were bleeding too.

"If you were with us, your people would no longer be in danger," her mother said. "What do you think kept you safe all these years, my daughter? Join me. You'll understand."

The fight left her.

Maybe I should just join them.

Heat at her neck, pulsing and white-hot, tore her from the reverie. Blinking, she looked down toward the pouch containing the heartseed. Intrinsically, she knew it wanted to be planted.

Where?

From inside the bushes, Alastor's tail twitched. His two-colored eyes snapped open.

"*Listen to your heart*," Alastor wheezed.

Kassia squeezed her eyes shut as the witches continued to chant around her. She drowned out all the noise, save the thumping of her own heart that beat in time with the pulsing seed around her neck.

My heart?

Images of the heartwood trees driving stakes through the Speakers swirled through her mind.

The heartseed was the key to the entire protection network, but it needed a heart.

After weeks of searching the continent for the answer, it all made sense. If only she had the strength left to do what must be done. Weakly, Kassia tried to lift her hand and tug against the bloodrose vines, but it was no use. She couldn't reach the seed.

Kassia lifted her chin to the dawn skies above. "I'm not strong enough. I'm so sorry. I tried."

Her head lolled forward. Her chin rested against her chest, and as the magic poured from her body, green lights surrounded her. Kassia had nothing left to give.

"*My dear, you are more than strong enough.*"

"Grandmother?" Kassia whispered, surprise flooding her voice. "I can't do this alone."

"*Oh, my dear granddaughter, you're never alone.*"

Kassia lifted her head to find the field had filled with glowing, white, translucent apparitions. Her grandmother was there with the other Speakers. All of her ancestors going back thousands of years were with her. The malefic witches didn't react, didn't see them as they continued their evil chants.

Lorayne whispered, "*You were born for this, to protect the people no one else thinks of. It is your destiny. It always was.*"

The spirits began to link hands, forming a network of magic that poured directly into her chest. She gasped.

"Join us," the malefic witch said, gripping her throat again, hissing spittle into her face, oblivious to the magical forces at play.

"I'll never join you," Kassia screamed, praying that all the feral, nature gods could still hear her. "I would rather die."

"Then die." Her mother released her with a cackle and joined the chanting.

She truly is gone.

Exhaling, slow and deep, Kassia steeled herself. Twisting her body, she used all her remaining strength to rip her wrist free. The vines resisted at first, but the thick layer of blood coating her skin gave just enough room for her hand to start to slide free. She ripped again, screaming and twisting. All at once, it gave way.

Thaen stood just outside the circle, bark climbing up his face as he fought back the vines. His hands dropped, and he ducked behind a building to dodge a bolt of dark magic hurling toward him, but it was enough.

In a quick movement, Kassia freed the blade from her boot and, without pausing to think, drove the knife into her chest and wrenched it down to open a gash. Pulling it free, she allowed it to go tumbling across the cobblestones as she grasped the pouch at her neck.

With a scream, Kassia shoved the heartseed through her chest and into her own heart.

Heartwood Roots

Chapter Twenty

Witches lurk these woods.

— *Whispers of the wind.*

Power flared to life within Kassia as the seed woke. Roots wove out of her heart, growing between her ribs and nestling along her spine. Blinding pain ripped screams from Kassia's mouth as the heartseed took hold deep in her chest. Magic tendrils accompanied the physical, searching for the sprawling web of magic stemming from the heartwood trees connected to the Tangled Root. And then the protection from all those planted seeds being nurtured by the wildecraft of witches snapped into place.

"Hold her!" a malefic witch called.

"Drain her now!" her mother demanded.

Kassia rose, and the witch's vine snapped free of her other hand. The ones holding her feet withered to ash as their spell wavered.

"Attack!" a voice shouted from the tree line.

Turning, Kassia glimpsed a group of a dozen men and women charging from the nearby forest toward the malefic witches. Her eyes watered as she realized that they'd come back for her.

No magic.

No power.

They'd still returned for their own.

Hissing wickedly, Alastor burst forth from the bush to slide to a stop at Kassia's side. Relief that the little cat was all right flooded her. Thaen stepped out from behind her burning cottage, covered in dark blood not his own.

A purple-edged portal slashed to life, and wildecraft witches, all chanting and holding hands, stepped out of the slit in the air behind Adonis. Wrenn, Gwinifer, and Delphia joined—determined and angry expressions on their faces. They wielded crystals, bones, and stick charms as they rejoined their sister.

They came for me.

A hex from the wildecraft witches spiraled toward the malefics, interrupting their incantations, and the green trickle of magic from Kassia's mouth ceased.

Five malefic witches remained, their sisters fallen around them. Her mother stood in the center. They'd abandoned the spell aimed at Kassia and now hurled their own magics at their new enemies. It wouldn't matter.

Kassia's grandmother stood beside her, a steely gaze in her eyes. "You are the product of a thousand generations of witches, each growing stronger than the last. You were made for this."

Spirits of her ancestors and the heartwood witches hovered behind her, holding her up, promising that she was not alone. Lifting her hands, Kassia tapped into that energy, too.

"What are you doing?" her mother screamed.

Kassia lifted her hands. "I'm sorry to do this to you, but you didn't heed the warnings. Death will cleanse you, and I hope you find peace."

A burst of protection shot out of her palms, pure, unfiltered energy from the heartwood spell. It struck each of the malefic witches straight in their twisted hearts, and they fell without another sound. The ground opened up and swallowed their corpses.

Kassia snarled as she looked toward the east, toward the dark goddess, Niamh. “Let this be a warning to you and your witches. These woods are protected.”

The Heart of the Forest

Chapter Twenty-One

Magic springs from the heart.

— *Grimoire of the Wildegrove witch, Kassia Guara.*

Flowers braided in her hair, Kassia exited the magic doorway in the garden where she'd hidden her grimoire. She walked toward the little cottage tucked between the midnight poppies and nightflame blooms as the heartseed twined deeper around her heart. Alastor trailed her, her constant shadow.

"*It is good to protect the knowledge while malefic witches are in the woods,*" he said.

"Are there more?" she asked.

"*Many.*"

"Then we'll deal with them," she replied.

The protection network connecting the roots of the heartwood trees pulsed with magic under their feet, and she could feel its energy in her chest with every step. And within, the spirits of her grandmother and mother resided.

Thaen hopped down from the roof and wiped sweat onto his

sleeve. "The roof is nearly fixed. The thatching suffered the worst of it, as the walls are all stone. By tomorrow, it'll be good as new."

"Thank you for helping," she replied. "I'm so glad that we were able to save it."

Losing the cottage would've been a terrible blow with all the rebuilding that the village was already undertaking. She thanked the forest gods that the damage to her cottage had been minor and that the other Speakers had sent aid to help the village with repairs.

"Of course." His hands found hers gently as he looked deeply into her eyes. "I find you captivating. I know there are obstacles, but we could at least try and see what there is."

"You're the chieftain, in the middle of a war," she said. "Your people will need you."

Thaen tilted his head, his long, black hair falling against his shoulder. "What is the point of all of this if we don't fight for our happiness?"

She'd always been comfortable in his company, at ease and strangely happy. Even through her grief, he sparked happiness inside her. When he said he wouldn't just give up on them, she believed him.

"I would like to try," she admitted as a blush crept across her dark skin.

Thaen wrapped his arm around her waist and pulled her against his chest. "I need to be getting back to the Seven Forests. Adonis has graciously agreed to portal me. He should be getting here any mo—"

Adonis trudged through the long grasses in his robes. "Are you ready?"

Thaen cast a sly look toward the sorcerer. "If my people need me to return anytime I am visiting with you, I'll simply send a quick raven over to Adonis, and then he can pop open a portal and bring me back."

Adonis cast an exasperated look back toward the naturalist warrior. "I will help in times of need." And then he mumbled something under his breath about wasted talents.

"Excellent!" Thaen grinned. "I'll get some defensive measures in place back home and check on the seed. I'll be back in a week and stay for a fortnight. Adonis has already agreed to meet me at the Way if I bring him some specimens for his sorcery." Thaen pulled her into a quick kiss. "And then perhaps you can join me for a few weeks."

She pressed a kiss against his lips before detangling herself from his bark-skinned arms. "Looking forward to it."

"Nothing so insignificant as distance could keep me from you," he said before following the sorcerer down the road.

It wasn't a declaration of love, but it was a commitment to see this through without allowing excuses to hinder them. And it was perfect.

He waved before disappearing from her sight.

Smiling to herself, Kassia took a birch broom and began to sweep the dead vines and ash from her stoop. When it was brushed clean, she stepped inside the cottage to look at her growing stash of charms, spelled herbs, potions, and tomes.

Breathing softly, she leaned forward on the shop counter, tracing the protection web spreading through the roots of the heartwood trees all across the continent. She felt before she heard the footsteps of a customer.

A middle-aged woman, propped up on a crutch, pushed open the door to the cottage. Kassia recognized her at once.

"Mairwen, how are you? How is the leg healing up?" Kassia asked.

"Good! Running halfway to Rodarri on it didn't help, but I've been staying off it since. It doesn't hurt anymore."

"Wonderful," Kassia said. "Are you here for a checkup?"

"I was hoping you had more of the heartwood protection charms?"

Kassia smiled. "Yes. I have harvested a few."

Reaching up to a high shelf, she slipped a single heartwood pendant on a leather strap out of the spelled box. She handed Mairwen the charm.

Kassia instructed, "Wear it always and be sure to bring it into the sunlight and give it fresh spring water often. Good women, great witches died so we might have these. Every splinter is precious, so please take good care of it."

Mairwen looped the charm over her neck, glancing around the cottage. "It must get lonely here being by yourself after your dear grandmother passed."

Kassia smiled, sensing the beating of the heartseed in her chest connecting her to other witches, the steady pulsing in the roots of the land, the whispering winds, and the rustle of her familiar prowling the forest.

"I'm never alone."

Epilogue

A witch is never afraid of the woods.

— *Fairy Tale of the Crescent Moon Witch.*

The goddess, Niamh, sat atop her raised dais on a violet crystal throne, beneath the layers of diaphanous veils and white, smoky incense. The air crackled with the foreign magics she'd brought to this world, which extended outward and connected her to her faithful by purple ropes of energy. She dragged her long fingertips across the armrest and bit back a snarl. Days ago, ten ropes had snapped, and she demanded answers.

The doors to the inner sanctum opened as three witches entered. Reaching the foot of the dais, they bowed. As one, they rose. Their skin was pocked with branches that grew outward, too many eyes, and small, corrupted creatures that had made their bodies home. It was the price of the power they wielded.

"You called for us, goddess?" the first malefic witch inquired.

"What happened to my witches?" Niamh hissed. "I have thirteen covens in Teridar, and now one is missing."

"We tracked their energy signature to the Wildegrove," another witch replied. "We found no bodies, but that is where their energy ended."

"What killed an entire coven?" Niamh tapped the armrest in anger. "My own blood ran through their veins, mixed with the magics of Etheria. They should have been able to stand against nearly all threats."

"It was the wildecraft witches, goddess," the first witch answered. "They have created protections using heartwood. Somehow, it spans the continent, connecting witches across the nations. We have yet to find a way to break it."

"Trees?" Niamh hissed again. "My witches are dead from trees?"

The third witch licked her sharpened teeth. "There is a powerful witch in the Wildegrove, the center of all their power. She is protecting the villages and the spell that is keeping us out."

Niamh's temper flared. "So kill her."

"Our sisters tried and failed," a witch answered. "For now, the Wildegrove is protected."

Niamh's laugh echoed against the carved stone walls. "For now."

Afterword

Thank you for reading!

If you enjoyed *The Wildegrove Witch* please consider leaving a review on Goodreads or Amazon. Reviews, ratings, and word of mouth are so important for independent authors. Every review helps. If you haven't yet read the main series, check out *The High Seer*.

For more information about upcoming works and updates, visit my website www.alexbreewrites.com or follow me on Instagram @alex.bree.writes.

Want to stay up to date? Sign up for my author newsletter for exclusive updates, sneak peeks, and release news.

Alex Bree is a fantasy author and attorney living in Meridian, Idaho, with her husband, children, and dog.

ACKNOWLEDGMENTS

This was such a fun story to write! Combining dark fantasy with cottagecore vibes was a natural pairing in this high fantasy world that's bursting with magic.

Thank you to my husband, Korey, who has been my ultimate supporter, first alpha reader, and brainstorm partner. You listen to all my insane musings, first drafts, editing and revising woes, bad poetry attempts, and you never question when the writing process gets weird (and it does). To my children, I love you and can't wait until you're old enough to read this!

Thank you to my writing group partners. You're the first ones I go on artwork, artists, editors, blurbs, chapter titles, website design, social media posts, fonts, formatting, obscure grammar questions, and everything else. I wouldn't want to do this without you all. Thank you: AJ Braun, Billie Grey, Loren Huxley, Maia James, Jaci M. Lunera, PC Nottingham, Tiffany O'Haro, N.C. Scrimgeour, Nico Vincenty, and Kaela Woodruff.

Special thanks also go to my wonderful friends who have encouraged and supported me: Taylor, Cailin, Jaime, and Ruth.

Finally, to all those of you who read and enjoyed this book—I want to thank *you*. This would not exist without your continued support.